Give Me Your Answer, Do

Give Me Your Answer, Do

Peter Marchant

Tough Poets Press
Arlington, Massachusetts

Copyright © 1960 by Peter Marchant

Cover artwork: *White Horse* (detail)
by Joris Hoefnagel (1542-1601)

ISBN 979-8-218-06151-7

This edition published in 2022 with permission from the Estate of Peter Marchant by:

Tough Poets Press
Arlington, Massachusetts 02476
U.S.A.

www.toughpoets.com

To Marguerite Young
P.L.M.

Chapter One

I

At the office Miss Finlay was something of a dark horse. Though it was usual in the typists' room of Messrs Boothby, Gold & Co., of Fenchurch Street, London, for everyone to know everything about everyone, no one knew a thing about Miss Finlay simply because she never discussed her private life. She had been with the firm twelve years, during which time an absolute Noah's Ark of shorthand typists had tripped into the office, had exchanged the secrets of their separate bosoms, and had departed—knitting bags crammed with the hoarded rubbish of their desks—their separate ways. Miss Finlay remained a mystery, but a mystery arousing little or no curiosity. If she didn't talk about her private affairs or her love life, there was, poor thing, an obvious explanation.

Her own mother could hardly have described her as attractive, even if she had wanted to. Miss Finlay was tall and ungainly, with large feet and hands which made sudden, gawky movements. Her hair was flat, her upper teeth protruded, and she wore spectacles with plain, tortoise-shell rims. Her complexion was of that high colour that prohibits the use of cosmetics, and her nose was inclined to be shiny. It could always be said of her that she looked clean and neat, as if she scrubbed herself very regularly with carbolic soap; but this very English virtue was not one that the powdered and painted girls of the typists' room particularly admired. Her clothes were sensible, and she wore no gew-gaws; on her wrist was an inexpensive wristwatch with a large, masculine face.

Miss Finlay was neither liked nor disliked by the girls, for she never took part in their feuds, never made spiteful remarks, and always remained politely aloof when they chattered scandal. When it was her turn to make tea, she made the tea rather well; when one of the girls wished to leave the office early, she would always take over undone work without complaint. Her voice, whilst not being remarkable either for its beauty or its ugliness, was somewhat Girls' Public-school, and therefore excellent material for the office mimics. She arrived every morning on the dot of nine-thirty, summer and winter, fair weather or foul, and except when the roads were slippery with snow or ice, she invariably travelled on a green sports bicycle with drop handlebars. This she kept in top-notch condition, parking it during the day in the tiled corridor on the ground floor for all to see and admire. Whence she came no one knew, nor whither she returned.

When new girls arrived at Boothby's, greedy for fresh confidences, they spent a while speculating about the mystery of Miss Finlay, but since there was no information, their curiosity soon died—their own lives were obviously ever so much more interesting.

II

It was the eve of Easter Bank Holiday, and throughout the City there was an air of excitement. That Thursday afternoon dragged through three usual days in as many hours, in spite of the tea-breaks that were as frequent and as prolonged as possible so that everyone's holiday plans could be made known and exclaimed over *ad nauseum*.

In Boothby's typists' room, *fourses* started at three-thirty and lasted till nearly five. The senior typist, a tall, sophisticated cosmopolitan, who had once been the spouse of a Mr Fleisch who was never discussed, produced a tin of somewhat dubious foreign biscuits with a great jangling of bracelets, and offered them around.

"Miss Finlay, you will take one, no?"

"Gosh, thanks awfully—jolly decent of you!"

Miss Finlay plunged a large, pink hand into the tin, and almost knocked it to the floor. Mumbling apologies, she, turned from her natural shrimp to lobster, involuntarily grimaced at Mrs Fleisch, and tried to cover her confusion by taking a somewhat ferocious bite of a biscuit hard as a bathroom tile.

Gladys Peach, at twenty-two plump as a duckling, doted on goodies, and dimpled charmingly as she accepted hers.

"Thanks very much, I can't resist," she cooed. "What are they, Nola?"

"They are *knackerlie*, and they are coming all the way from Frankfurt," Mrs Fleisch replied. "Norma, you will take one, please?"

"Thanks ever so," Norma Gracewell whined. She was seventeen and a half, the junior of the typists' room, but tough as telegraph wire and a jazz fiend. Gladys Peach thought her common because of her accent, her smeary lipstick, her incessant gum chewing, and her ability to eat huge lunches five times a week apparently without gaining an ounce. Norma sniffed loudly at Mrs Fleisch's offering before dunking it into her tea.

"They 'aven't 'arf got a funny smell," she said, "it's just like being in one of them old churches."

"*Those* old churches," said Gladys, sticking out her little finger, and sipping and nibbling alternately, genteel as an Embankment pigeon.

Mr Bacon, the insurance clerk, a battered Yorkshireman with a large, reddish nose, thinning sandy hair, and pink-rimmed blue eyes, banged into the typists' room with a sheaf of invoices. He was all ready to go on stage as *Baron Stonybroke* in any production of "Cinderella" from Hammersmith to Scarborough, which was the main reason, perhaps, that he had the reputation for being the office comic. He was also said to drink more beer than the whole of Boothby's staff combined.

"Na then, lassies," he bantered, "stop the hen-party and let's get a little work done. Women are all the same, natter, natter, natter from morn till night. It's just as well you've got a coop to yourselves, if you ask me."

"No one's asking you," responded Miss Gracewell, "so you can keep your trap shut."

"Na, then, lass, I'm old enough to be your dad, and I'm not above giving you a good smacked bottom at that, so you'd best keep a civil tongue in your head. Now, what I'd like to know is what you're all going to do over Easter."

He looked sidelong at Miss Finlay, who at once began busily to clean her typewriter.

"Well, I never," Gladys Peach coyed, "I do believe you're as much a gossip as we are, Mr Bacon."

"'Course he is," said Norma. "Men are all the same: they accuse women of being gossips, and they're the biggest gossip-cats of the lot. 'Aven't you learnt anything from that fyancee of yours?"

"You girls, you are making excursions, no?" interjected Mrs Fleisch diplomatically.

"What's that? Sounds filthy to me," Norma guffawed.

"Everything sounds filthy to you, Norma," jabbed Gladys, "and we all know why. Well, if no one's going to tell what they're doing over Easter, I'll tell—so there!"

"I'm not doing anything very special," Norma responded. "Joe's not got leave from Germany, so I expect I'll just go out with the gang. Tonight it'll be the Palais 'cos there's a Gala night and tomorrow we'll probably go for a ramble in the country. Jimmy Cochrane asked me to go to Southend with him on the back of his motor-bike, but I don't think I will. It's all right while he keeps going, but when we stop all he ever talks about is piston-rings. It's ever so boring."

"I had a motor-bike when I was in the Navy," commented Mr Bacon, "but I can't say as ever I talked to me pillion about piston-rings when we stopped—not for longer than was decent in any case."

"Ow, shut up," said Norma, "you're a proper caution, reelly you are."

Miss Finlay's "A" key was slightly out of true, so that occasionally it jammed. She manipulated it back into position with a pair of tweezers she kept in the left-hand drawer of her desk for just that purpose; then she wiped the tweezers on a Kleenex and replaced them. The typists' room *badinage* was just a bore, and so was Norma Gracewell's wretched gang. She could just picture them on their ramble: slick-haired, spindle-legged boys in corduroy shorts, and screeching girls with fat buttocks in those frightful jeans—they were trampling down her beloved England, defiling "the mountains green" with pop-bottles, ice-cream cartons, and orange peel, and making pastures that had been pleasant and lovely, sleazy with their messiness. If only they weren't all so messy, if only they were less ugly, she might have brought herself to forgive them.

"What are you doing, Nola?" Gladys Peach asked Mrs Fleisch—Gladys was intent on picking up biscuit crumbs with a moistened forefinger, and placing them on the tip of her pale tongue.

"I make an excursion with a friend formerly from Frankfurt. He lost everything, but everything, through Hitler, and last year his wife is running away from him. But now once more he is very rich, since he manufactures jewellery—Mrs Fleisch had guarding her ear-lobes two milk-bottle tops, and these she touched lovingly for a moment before continuing. "He takes me to Maidenhead in his car—I have not seen this Maidenhead, but I have heard much from it."

"By goom," commented Mr Bacon, giving the rest a broad wink, "if you're going to let him take you on the river in a punt, you'd best watch out for yourself, Mrs Fleisch."

"Thank you, Mr Bacon, but I think you have no worry. Unfortunately, I am not more a chicken."

Mrs Fleisch, Miss Finlay decided, would wear a black satin dress with a high Germanic collar, and geometric apertures of black net above the chest. For the journey she would be wrapped in a slightly mangy fox cape smelling of moth-balls, and at luncheon she would drape it elegantly over the back of her chair, and flash her long yellow teeth in a brilliantly *temperamentvoll* smile. Her escort had a droop nose and a charcoal jowl, and when he gesticulated he displayed a thick gold ring with a diamond. He was doing the ordering with the air of one who knew every *maitre d' hotel* from Maidenhead to pre-revolution Moscow intimately—a patron of fine cuisine, a *gourmet*—yet the lunch was still Brown Windsor soup, followed by roast mutton and over-boiled cabbage...

"Well, tell us what you're doing, Glad," asked Miss Gracewell.

"Well, tonight my fiongcee George is taking me to the *Coliseum* to see "Tears Where My Heart Was" which everyone says is just too marvellous; and tomorrow we're going down to Hove by the *Brighton Belle* and we're staying over till Monday when

George's parents, Mr and Mrs Sneath, are coming down just for the day by car, and we'll drive back with them."

"Cor luv a duck, you aren't half going it," Norma giggled; "Brighton for a dirty week-end, well I never!"

"We're staying in separate hotels if you want to know, and it's Hove, not Brighton, and I think you have the nastiest mind I've ever come across."

Miss Finlay knew that Gladys' George was a bank clerk, eight pounds ten a week, minus Pay-as-you-earn and National Health; thin, tall, and knobbly, with hands that were clumsy with teacups but good at carpentry, cars, and tomato growing. He would be bored stiff at the *Coliseum*, but Gladys would weep copiously into his handkerchief with the utmost enjoyment, and that would be his reward. A pat or two on his hand in addition, perhaps, and certainly a fair performance of the dimples. Gladys would eat a pound of milk chocolate creams while she wept, leaving the hard ones for George. Tomorrow she would wear a flowered print too small for her and much too summery, and George would have to take off his sweater for her on the beach, and take her to a tea-shop where she would eat about four chocolate éclairs. George thought her wonderful, and as sweet as a kid sister. In ten years time she would weigh a good twenty pounds more than he, but George would have for consolation a scrawny carrot of a son just like himself, and a marshmallow daughter, a miniature of Gladys; and then, of course, there would be his well-tended garden—wallflowers and antirrhinums in the front, and cabbage, lettuce, and tomatoes in the back . . .

"What's Miss Finlay doing over the holidays?" Mr Bacon asked—he gave her a quick glance to observe her reaction as he spoke.

Miss Finlay jerked up her cup, swallowed some tea the wrong way, spluttered, and replaced the cup in the saucer with a crash.

She occupied herself rolling a sheet of letter heading over two carbon copies into her machine.

"I—I don't expect I'll be doing anything very much," she said, and began to type at about a hundred and twenty a minute.

The ladies of the typists' room silently agreed.

III

Miss Finlay started to cycle back to her bed-sitting-room in Victoria rather less buoyantly than usual. Once or twice recently she had felt that heaviness of the heart that hadn't troubled her since she'd left school. She was at a loss to understand the cause. She had before her four days of holiday, four days of blessed privacy and lovely freedom, during which she could ride into the depths of Epping Forest, to the soaring spires of Ely, to the grace and splendour of Wells, to Land's End in the far west, or wheresoever else her heart most desired; yet she felt a twinge of anguish that was like a premonition of evil.

Held a prisoner in a Fenchurch Street traffic jam, a bus, huge and impassable to the front, and a sleek black limousine, sinister and ruthless, to the right; forced to wait with one foot on the crowded pavement, she tried to explain her *malaise*. The trouble was hardly the typists' room, surely. She had no wish to go rambling with Norma and the gang, or to Brighton with Gladys' George, or to Maidenhead with Mrs Fleisch's continental friend, did she? Emphatically not! In that case, what did she want to do?

She would begin by cooking herself a special supper: a nice, meaty lamb chop with a well-browned pork sausage, a crisp rasher of bacon, a grilled tomato, some fresh-frozen peas, and some creamy mashed potatoes. Afterwards she would brew a good cup of tea to sip by the gas-fire—because it was still chilly in the evenings even if it was spring—and she would plan an itinerary for herself, her paint-box and her bicycle, for the next morning. And if there was still time, she might make a start on the landscape that had been at the back of her mind all day long: the front view of a horse looking over a gate with rolling downs in the background.

The bus in front started, allowing her to escape. Skilfully she wove in and out of the slow-moving, cumbersome traffic, till she was up to, then through, the traffic lights; and she flew westwards, feeling once more that swiftness and lightness that gave her—above the wretched humanity scurrying underground—the sublimity of a charioteering goddess.

Chapter Two

I

Miss Finlay had taken all of ten years to feather her nest—ten years of patient saving, and then waiting to find the precise article to suit her. Most people wouldn't bother so much about the quality of absolute rightness in so simple a utensil as a frying pan, or a breakfast cup, but then their carelessness could not but show in everything they did. Miss Finlay had always been fastidious, and she was rightly proud of it; her just reward was a little thrill of satisfaction and pride whenever she thought about the private snuggery she had made for herself, all the comfy seclusion that she had dreamed about for so weary a time . . .

She saw herself as a schoolgirl—M. standing on the seat of the loo looking out through the narrow window, loophole of her fortified tower, at the great chestnut trees, branches flecked bright green against the olive downs. The trees were beautiful, soaring high above the sharp-toothed ferrets, the vicious grey rats, that swarmed and gnawed at their roots.

"If only they'd leave me alone; if only they'd leave me alone . . ." Girls banging desks; girls whispering; girls giggling; girls with bright, mad eyes searching for M.'s corner, and planning sudden destruction from behind grubby hands . . .

"Catch, Margaret!" Monica Humphries, the mortal enemy of flaming hair and laughter sharp as broken glass—the ink-soaked paper missile that hit her cheek, spattering her Saturday clean blouse.

"Oh poor old rabbit, I've gone and made you piebald." "Throw it back at her, Magsie, don't be funky, throw it." "Rabbit's a coward, Rabbit's a coward . . ."

Miss Lambert at the door, and the class silent. "Good morning, girls." "Good morning, Miss Lambert." "This morning I'm going to dictate some notes on the vegetation of Equatorial Africa—Margaret Finlay, you're absolutely filthy. Go and wash your face this minute, and tonight you can write out one hundred times, 'I must wash my hands and face before I come to class' . . ."

"If only they'd leave me alone, I'd be happy for the rest of my days . . ." The loo a nun's cell. Sling a hammock from the water pipes; buy two or three eiderdowns, a carpet, maybe, and a picture or two to cheer up the drabness of the ochre walls; and an electric hotplate for cooking. Get supplies from the village—order them on a telephone and haul them up in a basket by a rope and pulley. Put a wash-basin in the corner, and always have a big cake of *Lifebuoy's Carbolic* that not a soul else could touch. Have a hanging bookshelf: *Alice*, of course, and *What Katy Did*, and *Black Beauty, King Arthur and his Knights, Treasure Island, A Child's Garden of Verses, The Arabian Nights* and *Mrs Beeton's Household Management*. Have a big new paint-box, and a really huge sketching-block . . .

"Who's in there?" "Me, Matron." "Who's me? Margaret Finlay?" "Yes, Matron. Please, Matron, I've got diarrhoea." "Well, you had better come to the sick-room for some medicine at once and then hurry back to class. I'm always finding you in the toilet during class-time, Margaret Finlay: if it happens again, you'll go straight to the Headmistress."

But now Margaret Finlay had her own little room, and Matron and the Headmistress and Monica Humphries and the whole bang lot of them were locked out. Good riddance.

Dear little room, with its white walls, canary yellow curtains and matching bedspread; the rust armchair that she herself had covered, and the rust, yellow and grey cushions that she herself had stitched; the grey Wilton carpet—a year's savings; the white bookcase and varnished walnut coffee table—night-school carpentry three winters ago; the massive oaken wardrobe and dining table—purchased for a song in a junk-shop in the Buckingham Palace Road, and refurbished at home. And her latest acquisition, Margaret Finlay's Christmas present to M., a great table radiogram of shiny walnut, which did justice, at last, to M.'s favourite record. Of course, she had a few other records now, but she didn't waste too much money on them, because every week she visited Westminster Public Library, where she could borrow them free.

Her kitchen consisted of a portable Belling Cooker on a marble-topped commode—a most convenient arrangement, and surprisingly adaptable to some fairly elaborate dishes. In the drawers of the commode were some fine silver cutlery and part of a set of Minton china—both these a legacy from Grannie Finlay—the only part of the past that did her any good. And in the commode's cupboard were two heavy, cast-iron frying pans, three thick saucepans of graduated size, and an excellent earthenware casserole. This was the modest extent of her *batterie de cuisine*, but it sufficed. She loved good food, which had never failed to soothe her and give her solace, and she had had enough of "simple but wholesome" fare at school and in hostels to last her a lifetime. Only after years of watery cabbage, underdone boiled potatoes, gristly meat, and overdone rice pudding, could anyone truly appreciate the privilege of well-cooked and imaginative eating in privacy, with a book or magazine for company.

Yes, now Margaret Finlay had nearly all the comfort she wanted, but she had worked hard to achieve it. When she had first undertaken the venture of a bed-sitting-room to herself, the place had looked very different . . .

The naked electric bulb had draggled like an unhealthy weed from the cracked ceiling; there were naked rectangles on the mud-coloured walls where pictures had hung. It was the sort of room where someone might have hanged herself! She could see the body swinging from the water-pipe, the face livid as cheese, the eyes suffused with blood . . . "Come off it, M., you're getting morbid and making yourself all windy. Soap, water, and new paint will work wonders. Buy some furniture, a carpet, and so forth; make some curtains and stuff: 'make-do-and-mend' and that sort of thing. And just think of getting away from the hostel."

That hostel! Would she ever forget it?

"Magsie, may I come in for a minute? I promise I won't stay long, but I've had the most heavenly letter from John which I must read you; and look, he's sent a photo of himself in uniform! Isn't he madly good-looking? and the whole thing is he simply hasn't a clue that he is. That's why I'm so nuts about him I suppose! Do listen to this, Magsie, it's an absolute *scream*! The tent collapsed in the middle of the night . . ."

What was that silly girl's name? Every week it was a letter from someone else that had to be read out loud—John, Frank, David, Keith—and she always said she would just stay a minute, and two hours later would still be there gabbling. But she wasn't the worst: what about the organisers that would never take no for an answer . . .

"May I come in for a moment, Finlay? We're getting together a party to go for a hike to St Albans this Saturday. Crookham is coming—she's bringing the Matthews girl whom I can't stand; but Crookham insists, so let her cook her own goose, I say, I don't give a damn. Isabel's coming with me, and we thought it might be a good show if you came with someone—you know, not being a snob or anything, but it *is* different being with one's own sort.

We thought we would make our own chow—take along some equipment in rucksacks. I say, Finlay, you simply must come with us—it's jolly unhealthy for you to be on your ownsome all the time..."

So the top front room at 80 Ebury Street had acquired a new tenant, who, from the moment the windows were covered with blinds, had loved it and cherished it. For Margaret Finlay, a room of her own had meant that for her, at last, life had begun.

II

She washed her face with her nice green flannel, combed her hair, and set about preparing dinner. She ate it—as she had promised herself—sitting snugly by the gas-fire, and very delicious it was. After she had washed the dishes, she brewed herself a pot of *Earl Grey*, and settled down in the armchair once more, this time with her A.A. road map in her lap instead of her plate, to plan her Easter expedition.

If she went to Ely, just for example, she could travel, either up the Great North Road via Baldock, or she could go by Bishop's Stortford and Newmarket, perhaps making a digression on the way to Saffron Walden—where she had never been, but had always wanted to because of the name. The Great North Road would be much more direct, of course, but would it be as interesting? The Great North Road was a wee bit lonely...

Gladys Peach was sitting next to George in the darkness, transfixed by the box of dreams before her, in which tears were always pleasurable because they were followed inevitably by a lovely reconciliation in a blaze of sunshine—the lovers united after all their tribulations. The curtain fell on their embrace, rose to find them bowing, and smiling brilliantly at the audience; they turned to each other with private smiles and knowing looks; the other characters lined up—more bows and smiles—the heroine blew kisses that could only spring from the certain knowledge she had that she and the hero would be happy ever after. This descent of the curtain was not death: it was an exclusion of the audience from the performers' private world of sunlight. Did Gladys feel excluded? No, she didn't, because she had her George looking at her with adoring eyes, and he was all ready to squeeze her plump little hand whenever she wanted. Gladys would never feel excluded from anything.

And Norma Gracewell? She was with the gang, sprawled around a table messy with empty Coca-Cola bottles, ash-trays full of cigarette stubs and globules of chewing gum. There was a smell of sour, unwashed bodies, and Woolworth's perfume—like the smell in the ladies' room at the skating-rink. They watched the contortions of jitterbugs under the glaring arc-lamps—or was the *Hammersmith Palais* dim, with violet and rose motes reflected by a glittering mirror globe? "Ever so romantic," Norma would say with a giggle.

The music was blaring: not a dignified English waltz, ladies in long dresses dipping and swaying in their gentlemen's arms like sea-gulls riding the waves, but a convulsive jerking of limbs like the keys of a teleprinter. A tall, gangling youth in an Edwardian suit, his jaws rotating gum, slid from his seat and looked at Norma with a knowing grin. "Norm" shrugged her bony shoulders and got up to join him. They writhed into the crowd of dancers and disappeared—like worms dropped into a bucket of worms. Ugh!

And Nola Fleisch? She was entertaining refugee friends in her Belsize Park sitting-room. There was a heavy smell of Continental cooking, and the windows were tight shut. Frau Fleisch served coffee, very black and full of grounds, with those adamantine biscuits she offered round the office this afternoon. Because it was the beginning of a holiday she'd made a very Fleisch-ish *torte*—mucilaginous mock cream, pink and green, on pastry like dusty typing-paper. They talked, sitting very upright and Germanic, with medicinally clean hands gesticulating, of—pre-war Frankfurt; the opera; *wunderbar* holidays and excursions; *wunderbar baden,* where *wunderbar* concerts were combined with *wunderbar* tables d'hôte, and even more *wunderbar* cures for gastronomic disorders; all in a world that had disappeared for ever, as certainly as Imperial Rome.

And of it, these sensual survivors—and droop-nosed, dark-jowelled Rudi giving Nola Fleisch furtive glances of desire, his black eyes glittering below chicken-skin eyelids. Fleisch's serpentine spine quivered with excitement as she watched him— reptile sensuality! Ugh!

Wasn't Margaret Finlay lucky to be sitting so cosily on her own, the gas-fire popping comfortably, but the air in the room wholesomely fresh, unbreathed by anyone but herself? Tomorrow she could get up at whatever hour she liked, and take off for Ely, Wells, John o' Groats, or the Himalayas—if such was her pleasure. She had to meet no one at a particular time, to catch a particular train to a particular destination. She was as free as air to voyage where she liked, to wear what she liked, to eat what she liked, and to dream such as her heart loved with no one's interference...

> There's a long, long trail a-winding
> Into the land of my dreams...

She saw herself pedalling up the Great North Road: a gaggle of cyclists were gaining on her from behind—she could hear their laughter mocking her slowness, and they jangled their bells at her contemptuously. They yelled, they cat-called, they whistled, because they were strong in companionship, and she was single. They were brutes! They were ugly, cruel, and beastly, and she was going to teach them a lesson that "he travels fastest who travels alone." She trod on the pedals with all her strength, her lungs gasping. The north wind thrust against her, and her heavy tweed skirt smothered her legs. The gang were gaining on her and gaining on her, and in the panic she had felt as a child in *Grandmother's Footsteps*, she knew she was defeated. They passed her with ease—such ease—and they forged ahead, piston buttocks disdaining her. The jangle dwindled into the distance. M., breathless and exhausted, took out a bar of chocolate—milk chocolate, with fruit and nuts—for consolation.

"I'm hungry," Miss Finlay muttered, "I just fancy a piece of chocolate—*Rowntree's Motoring* with fruit and nuts."

"Eat, eat, eat—go on, eat till you burst, like a frog blown up with air. Gorge yourself with food!" In ten years' time, M. would be encased in a great, fat woman's body, like an overcoat made of eiderdown; it would weigh her down so that she would have to walk up the easiest hills. In twenty years' time, M. would be drowned in a body as big as a whale's, like Jonah. "What will poor Robin do then, poor thing?"

The walls closed in. The air was suddenly stifling, though the hands and feet were like ice. The radio muttered from above; from outside in the street came the shrill voices of children at play; from the landing, there was the sound of the toilet; but in the room there was such stillness that these noises were no more than the tapping of fish colliding against the hull of a sinking submarine.

The wardrobe lowered towards her: the bookcase, the coffee table, the bed, even, in its bright yellow coverlet, were sinister, menacing, like . . . like . . .

The time the dolls had condemned M. to be taken from the nursery to a place of execution, and there be hanged by the neck until... Because M. had snatched up Marigold, the biggest of the dolls, to force her to be a good little girl...

"You're an ugly, beastly little tike and I hate you," M. had said, and had shaken Marigold furiously. But Marigold had done nothing but stare back, her eyes cold as glass, till M. had thrown her against the fender of the gas-fire to teach her a lesson, and then stamped on her head; and when they saw Marigold lying headless, all twisted up amongst the pieces of pink face, the dolls had held a trial, the nursery cupboard his Honour the Judge; and when they had condemned M. to death, M. had screamed, "I didn't mean it, I didn't mean it," till Miss Pritchard had come running in.

"Why, you naughty, ungrateful little girl, Margaret Finlay! You should be ashamed of yourself, smashing that beautiful doll that Mummy and Daddy gave you for your birthday. You're a spoilt horror and as a punishment you shall not play in the garden this afternoon. I shall lock you in your bedroom till you can learn to behave yourself, and what's more, you shall go without your tea. The destructiveness of the child! I've never known anything like it. One day, God will punish you, then you'll be truly sorry..."

Margaret Finlay, panic in her heart, groped her way to the radiogram. She turned it on with fumbling fingers, and put M.'s favourite record on the turntable. With heart palpitating, she fingered the needle till the sound rasped through the speaker, then she twisted the control switch. The record fell, the needle-arm swung over to the grooves. At last, M.'s tune came through to comfort and soothe her.

> Ride a cock-horse to Banbury Cross
> To see a fine lady upon a white horse...

The jog-trotting tune dispelled all the horror, until it all seemed comfortably ridiculous. The walls receded; the wardrobe subsided into passive amiability once more; the room regained its comfort and tranquility. Margaret Finlay played the record three times through; and by such simple magic, curled up in her armchair with her fingers pressed over her eyes, she completely recovered her natural high spirits.

III

Margaret Finlay rose from the armchair, and energetically assembled her painting gear on the coffee table, which she protected with two or three old copies of the *Sunday Express*. For company, she tuned into one of the weekly radio programmes that were as familiar as the typists' room conversations—without being nearly as offensive—and she settled down for a long evening of art.

To support the sketching block, she pressed her knees firmly together, splaying out her strong cyclist's legs for comfort. Her breathing soothed her with its regularity, and she held her tongue between her teeth—a sure sign of content. Then she lost herself in her work.

She was blocking in the horse that she wanted to paint a rich chestnut. She wanted him trotting towards her from a background of slightly misty olive downs. The downs and the sky she would suggest more than anything else, but the horse had to be very definite, very alive.

Now, she felt so much more relaxed that she could hardly recognise the panicky creature she had been not thirty minutes before. What a great goose she was, to let herself get all het up like that over nothing. She was nearly thirty-one—her birthday was May the 29th—and here she was, a great girl like her, behaving like a child of eight. It was absurd—in fact, it was simply . . . "ludicrous." So ludicrous that she had to smile at herself.

"Ludicrous" was a word she had learnt from Gran, only she had called it lud*r*icous, and even now there was a moment's hesitation—was it lu*di*crous, or not?—before she could write it.

"I cannot, I simply cannot, find my purse. It's too *ludicrous* never to be able to remember where one has put one's things from one moment to the next; and when I was your age, dear-heart, I had such a good memory. I'm getting old, I'm afraid. What a foolish old Grannie you have, dear-heart. Now where . . .? Too *ludicrous* . . ." "What does *ludricous* mean, Gran?" "It means I'm a silly old woman, dear-heart. Here we are, on the sideboard. Come on, now for the park."

They were going to watch the boats on the lake and buy ice-cream—that's why Gran wanted the purse. Strawberry ice running over the side of the cone, very cold, very sweet . . . just yummy. Gran, tall, white-haired, smelling of garden—her own garden—*lavender*—in a rustling black dress.

They'd just arrived from India, hadn't they? Mummy, Daddy, and Margaret. Was there anything left of India?—not really; she had been too young. There was a little, but it was frightfully vague . . .

A dusky face, a dear face, floating above her like a black moon after the good night kiss. The white curtains puff, then she was floating like a white cloud where the nasty flies couldn't eat her. A voice was singing—a dear voice . . .

And then?

They were on a ship that was tipping like a see-saw. Mummy was in a deck-chair with her eyes closed, her face grey as porridge, her dress yellow as egg. She jumped up and ran to the rails—to dive into the sea and become a mermaid? No, just to hang over the side and throw up like a fountain.

Daddy, 'starshes brown like his great, shiny horse, his hair burning like the sun just before it slid into the sea, carried her along the deck. He wore a collar of white cardboard and a black bow; Margaret was in her best dress, white, with a pink sash, and she had on her pink shoes.

"Gallop, Daddy, gallop, gallop, gallop." "After dinner, dearheart, if you're a very good girl and eat up all your vegetables." "But I don't like vegetables." "I know, but you must eat them just the same. If you want to grow into a big, strong girl, as tall as your daddy, you have to eat everything up."

After dinner. Margaret was on Daddy's shoulders, holding on to his ears, and he was galloping:

> Ride a cock horse to Banbury Cross
> To see a fine lady upon a white horse,
> Rings on her fingers and . . .

Lady in white uniform stopped them. "Excuse me, sir, your wife is asking for you." Daddy gave her to the lady, who had a chest covered with buttons that stuck into her. "Come along, Margaret, you come with me and let your daddy go to your mummy for a while."

"Be an extra specially good girl, and I'll come and say good night when you're in bed," Daddy called. She was an extra specially good girl, but Daddy never came.

Mummy was on deck in a white dress. She laughed like tinkling glass, her teeth were white, and her hair was as black and shiny as Ming's, her Burmese cat's. A lady in a hat like a white cloud bent down to whisper in Margaret's ear and blotted out the sun:

"You have a beautiful mother, little girl, but pray to God every night that you don't grow up like her." It must have been, Pray to God that you *do* grow up like her, it must have been! But it just didn't sound right if you didn't say "*Don't* grow up like her."

They were having tea in a big room with windows through which you could see the back of the ship, and the trail it left in the sea was like smoke, and the sea was cold and grey. Mummy was telling everybody about how she went hunting with Daddy, and how Daddy went and hid in a tree thinking it was the tiger; but it wasn't, it was only Mummy. Everyone laughed except Margaret because they thought Daddy was afraid, and Mummy laughed harder than anyone, and Margaret hated her because she knew that her Daddy wasn't afraid of anything.

"Then there was London and Gran," Margaret Finlay muttered out loud, and she held her picture at arm's length to appraise it. The horse was rather good, and she liked the colour—that excellent rich brown. It needed a lot more work on it yet, though.

Gran's. Daddy was singing in the bathroom, his face smothered in soap like whipped cream, and he winked at her in the mirror and waved his long-bladed razor with the black handle to conduct his own concert; his voice was loud and flat, and he cut a wide path of pink through the snow on his chin, and Grannie called, "Margaret" from the dining-room and she had to go. Daddy came in to breakfast smelling of soap, and his chestnut 'starshes, stuck out very straight and pointed, and he smelt of soap. He kissed Gran on each cheek, then he sat down at the head of the table, lifting Margaret on to his knees. He sang "Ride a cock horse," jogging her up and down; and when he came to "She shall have music wherever she goes," he shouted, and threw her into the air with his long, strong arms; the table stood on the ceiling, and her feet jumped over the tinkling birthday-cake light as if it were the moon and she the cow, and Gran laughed and scolded him for "letting the child's porridge get cold."

A shadow fell across them. Mummy came in to breakfast, her hair black as velvet and her nails as red as blood, and they all stopped talking and laughing—even Gran.

Gran's house was just like Gran, tall and thin, painted white outside, and inside dark and cool. Gran spoilt her, giving her big glasses of lemon-and-barley water clinking with big lumps of ice, and shiny black prunes from a big glass that stood on the tall sideboard in the dark, cool dining-room. And there were walks in the park to watch the boats or hear the band, and always ice-cream cones, and Gran would take her to the Peter Pan statue and tell her the story of the little boy who never grew up—it was Margaret's favourite, and Gran's too, so they had it over and over again.

Gran's house had a tiny front garden full of lavender, and a back garden with a very tall pear tree, and every morning she lifted Margaret up to feel if the hard fruit was ripening.

People kept on saying how hot it was, and how it was the best summer in years, but it never seemed very hot to Margaret: only very blue and clear, with sunlight glittering on white walls and dresses, and flashing fire from windows; and the grass was at first as green as the jade of Mummy's ring, which Margaret loved, and which Gran said she would get one day, when Mummy was dead. But then the grass dried up so that it looked just like the grass in India, and there was talk of drought, and they weren't allowed to water the poor flowers, or to fill the bath more than up to Margaret's thighs. Then it began to rain as if it was the flood, and the lawn became a sea of mud in which Margaret was not allowed to play. It was cold and grey outside, and they bought her a mackintosh, a sou'wester, and Wellingtons.

"Rain, rain, go away,
Come back on another day..."

The leaves from the pear tree were brown on the grey grass; fast flowing tears chased down the window-panes as if God were crying, and Margaret breathed out a mist. There were trunks and suitcases in the hall, and Margaret was in her new navy blue raincoat.

"Good-bye, dear-heart, take care of yourself and God bless you." Gran was kneeling down to kiss her, her blue eyes full of water, and she tightened her arms round Margaret and kissed her hard on the cheek over and over, and Gran's brooch stuck into Margaret like a sharp fork.

"Are we going away for long, Gran?" "You're going to live in the country, Margaret, like Daddy told you. There'll be cows and horses, pigs and chickens, and lots of new-laid eggs and cream." "Will there be a pear tree, Gran?" "Lots of pear trees, dear-heart, and apple trees, and plum trees." "Why don't you come, too?" "Because I live here in London, dear-heart." "Will you come and see me in the country?"

Gran looked funny.

"Perhaps, dear-heart, but in any case you'll come to London and visit me, I promise you. Then we'll go to the park, and we'll watch the boats on the Serpentine." "Gran, do let's. Can't I stay with you now, Gran?" "You must ask your mother, dear-heart."

Mummy was coming down the stairs in her fur coat, a red umbrella swinging from her wrist.

"Please, Mummy, may I stay with Gran?" "Don't be so silly, Margaret, of course you mayn't. You know we're going to live in Essex." "Will we be coming back for the holidays?" "Perhaps, we shall have to see. Now say goodbye to Gran properly, like a big girl. The car's waiting."

Gran twisted her hanky, looking at Mummy.

"Won't you let the child stay with me, at least over Christmas?" "I don't know, Gran. It's very kind of you, but we shall have to see that she settles down with the new governess first." "Surely it can't do her any harm to see her Grannie?" "All this moving about is so unsettling, don't you think, so we'll have to see. Good-bye, Gran, it's been very good of you to have us." "Well, Good-bye. You know . . . you know that I wish you and Gordon only well." "Of course. Come along, Margaret." "'Bye, 'bye, Gran." "'Bye, 'bye, dear-heart." Gran's face crumpled, and she turned away.

Aylestone Manor: a damp, grey house in a damp grey garden. Inside it smelt of old curtains and mildewed walls, and at night there were squeaks and bangs. Horrid house! Margaret wished and wished she were back in London with Gran, going for walks in the park, or sitting in front of the parlour fire telling stories, while the rain lashed the windows. Here she had a bath in a huge vat with great black scars, in a great, dark bathroom; then she had to run, shivering, to her horrid, cold bed in the great big nursery. And instead of Gran to make sure she'd dried herself properly, and to tuck her up warm and comfy under the bedclothes, and to tell her a story until gentle fingers pressed darkness over her eyes, there was Miss Pritchard.

Miss Pritchard's hand was all knuckles; her nose was as sharp and white as folded cardboard, and her neck was like a chicken's.

"Margaret, this is Miss Pritchard, your new governess."

"Hallo, Margaret, we're going to be good friends, I hope, aren't we?"

Miss Pritchard smelt of peppermint, and her clothes were mud coloured. Margaret hoped they were not going to be good friends. She wished Miss Pritchard would take up her black tin trunk, her blue hat-case, her black leather knitting-bag, and her brown umbrella, and go away in a taxi, never to return.

Miss Pritchard stayed.

A desert of endless grey days. Gran never came to see her, though she sent her a card with bright red and blue roses on it at Christmas; and a lovely woolly lamb, white, with black eyes and nose, and a red tongue, whom she called Peter, and took to bed every night. But she never saw Daddy, except on Sunday afternoons when she was dressed in her second best and had her hair tugged into curls and ribbons—which she *loathed*—to go down to the drawing-room to play for an hour, and to have tea with her parents. Mummy, stretched out on the sofa like a cat, watched whatever she did, while Daddy read one of those dreary papers about farming, with no pictures. Margaret *loathed* Sunday afternoon tea, even though there were always chocolate biscuits, and sometimes a coconut cake with a cherry on top.

From 9 till 12.30 every morning, Arithmetic, Geography, Grammar, and French, with Miss Pritchard rapping on the table that she was a naughty, stupid little girl who would never learn anything if she didn't concentrate instead of dreaming. In the afternoon, a walk to the village, with Miss Pritchard saying "Don't, Margaret," all the time, and pointing out flowers or trees or animals that Margaret had already noticed, and making a lesson of them. Tea at five o'clock in the nursery, then three-quarters of an hour's "Preparation" for her lessons in the morning, and a quarter of an hour's free time to play with her toys. Then bath, bed, and a mug of hot milk with skin wrinkling the top—which Miss Pritchard said was the best part, and insisted on stirring into the rest. Margaret could never decide which she hated more: the scummy hot milk, or Miss Pritchard.

"Good night, Margaret, sleep well." "Good night, Miss Pritchard, please may I have the door a bit open so that I can see the landing light?" "Certainly not, I've never heard of such nonsense. Go to sleep this instant, and don't fuss." "Why doesn't Daddy say good night to me any more?" "Because he's too busy, I expect. Now stop fussing and go to sleep."

"Margaret, you are *not* to be in the kitchen; now run along and play in the fresh air. Margaret, you are *not* to play in your mother's rose-garden, you know that as well as I do. Margaret, if

I catch you clambering over the rockery any more I shall have to report you to your mother: I've told you time and time again, and I'm getting tired of telling you. Margaret, don't answer them back: they're the village children and I've told you you're not to speak to them."

"Why mayn't I speak to them? Are they naughty?" "No, they're not exactly naughty . . ." "Then why mayn't I speak to them?" "Because—because they're rough." "How are they rough, Miss Pritchard? Do they play with knives and throw stones and spit?" "No, I don't think so." "Are they dirty?" "I don't really know, Margaret, do stop pestering me with questions." "But why mayn't I . . .?" "Because I say so, and because your mother says so. Let that be sufficient."

Tea parties with children of her own sort were, presumably, not rough. After lunch, a short rest, then getting ready: her best dress, clean white socks, and party shoes, and, finally, Miss Pritchard tugging at her straight hair with a wet comb.

"Margaret, will you kindly stop jerking your head away from me? How do you think I can make your hair look tidy if you keep on wriggling like an eel? Now don't forget to use your clean handkerchief, and don't forget to say Thank you for having me; and do try to join in with the games; Margaret, and don't make an idiot of yourself; and don't make a pig of yourself at tea—you're always so greedy that you make me ashamed. Margaret, will you keep still, or do I have to give you a good smacking?"

Arriving at the strange house, clutching Miss Pritchard's bony, gloved fingers with one hand, and with the other the present she'd had nothing to do with buying for the child she didn't want to give anything to. Miss Pritchard rang the front-door bell, Margaret's heart sank into her tummy and she suddenly wanted to go to the loo. The strange maid, the strange, dark hall, the strange smell of the strange house, and, worst of all, the noise of enemy-children shrieking and banging, and only a door between them and her. Without her overcoat, she was a snail without a shell. The present was her only protection, and that she had to give up.

"Many happy returns." "Thank you very much, you really shouldn't of; I say, what is it?" "It's a g-g-game..." "Oh, it's *Ludo*, that's the third *Ludo* I've been given this afternoon: I hate *Ludo*—I wish you could have made it ping-pong."

"Now, children, we're going to have *Musical Chairs*. As soon as the music stops, you must sit down, and the one left standing is out of the game. Now, one, two, three..."

> Here we go round the mulberry bush,
> The mulberry bush, the mulberry bush,
> Here we go round the mulberry bush
> On a cold and...

"It's Margaret, it's Margaret, she's always last." "Margaret Finlay, you must stand in the corner, dear, I'm afraid you're out..."

Two ladies, one in yellow with white flowers and a nose like a parrot's, the other thin and tall in black with a face as powdery as a doughnut, and they were talking about her, looking round to see she didn't hear, and their eyes looked nasty:

"... extraordinary how plain the child is—those rabbit-teeth and the squint eyes!" "The mother's a raging beauty, isn't she?" "Yes, if you admire that sort of beauty—I find it rather common, I'm afraid. She's got a shocking reputation, you know." "Yes, I know: we went to a hunt ball last week and Brenda Coulton told me—now run away and play with the other children, Keith, can't you see Mummy's talking?—now, where was I? Oh, yes, Brenda Coulton told me that..." "*Prends garde, la petite est là!*" A naughty look was on the parrot's face and the grown-ups suddenly took part in the children's game.

"Now, children, we'll split into two teams. I think we'll have Bruce for the captain of one team, because he's the birthday boy, and we'll let him choose the captain of the other team. Who shall it be? Rosemary? That's splendid! All right, Rosemary and Bruce pick sides. Rosemary, heads or tails?"

What can Mummy have been doing? Those ladies must have been talking about her, because everybody said how beautiful she was. Mummy must have been telling lies—what else could it be? Did Daddy know that she'd been naughty, or was he under a sort of spell? Perhaps that was it: he was under a spell because she was a witch, and everybody knew it except Daddy. Gran must have known it, which is why she seemed frightened whenever Mummy was there . . .

"Come on, Margaret, you're in my team, you're the last. Do play the game decently! Don't go and be a drip!" "Bruce, don't be rude to your guest—Margaret, dear, it doesn't matter your being last at all; someone must be chosen last, mustn't they? You'll be first next time, I expect. Now children, line up in your two teams. Now, you each get a ball, and you have to run to the door, leave it, and run back to your teams. The next one runs to the ball . . ."

So Mummy was a witch. She'd always known something was wrong somewhere. Miss Pritchard was one of her goblins—Mummy wanted to make sure that no one freed Daddy from the spell, and Margaret was the most dangerous person; that was why Miss Pritchard had to keep an eye on her. Well, Margaret would soon put an end to that sort of nonsense. She would find someone to help her against Mummy and Miss Pritchard—M.! M. was the invisible Margaret, who would spy on the enemy . . .

"Oh, come on Margaret, it's your turn! Oh, *do* come on, Margaret, run, will you . . ." "What do I do? I don't know what to do . . ." "Run and get the ball, Margaret! Ooh, Margaret, you've gone and spoilt *every*thing. You're such a drip! It's not fair. They've gone and won because we had the old rabbit—Rabbit Finlay . . ." "Bruce, I'm surprised at you! I thought you were a little gentleman, insulting a girl like that. Don't they teach you better than that at boarding-school? Apologise to Margaret!" "No, I won't, she's a drip. Rabbitty, Rabbitty Finlay, Rabbitty, Rabbitty Finlay . . ." "Bruce, you're a very nasty little boy, and I shall tell your father to give you a good hiding." "I don't care, I don't care; I shall never invite old Rabbitty to my party again . . ."

It was a horrid party, and Bruce was horrid, and dear God, please let Miss Pritchard come soon to take her home . . .

IV

Day after day of greyness and brownness, and the sun never shone. She was an ant crawling across a huge field of wet mud: she would never go to London to visit Gran, and Gran would never come down to see her, and nothing nice would ever happen again.

May the 29th—Margaret's birthday. She was having a horrible party in the nursery, and all the presents the other children had brought didn't make the children themselves any nicer. That Bruce wasn't there because he was at school; but Nancy Cudlip, a nasty fat girl, tore out Peter the lamb's black-button eyes. Keith Holliday broke nearly all her coloured chalks, and she hated him, even if he was the vicar's son. She hated them all, and she would have liked to throw all their presents onto a great bonfire.

Bed-time: Miss Pritchard's feet clicked briskly downstairs. Margaret was alone at last. She sat up in bed holding Peter the lamb; she kissed his poor blind eyes, and she hated and hated and hated Nancy Cudlip. She was wicked, and she would go to hell-fire, but she couldn't help it. She hated Miss Pritchard, too, and she hated Mummy. She hated everyone except Daddy, but he was under Mummy's *witch-spell*, and until someone set him free, no use to anyone. Would this be for always? Would no one ever go to the park to tell stories under whispering trees, or to lick strawberry ice-cream cones, watching the boats, ever again?

Margaret covered her face with the sheet and remembered Gran's lavender smell, and the sound of Gran's voice, as cool as a clear brook. It was as if Margaret died the day she left the tall, narrow white house. But even if Margaret was dead, there was M.!—M. was alive all right.

M. slid out of bed, took off Margaret's flannel nightie, and slipped Margaret's beastly braces from her teeth. M., freed from her ugly disguise, at last a pure and beautiful princess, knelt at the window praying to the moon with all her might to send her help and strength, that she might have the power to break the spell and destroy the witch, so that Margaret, Daddy, and Gran might all live together in the tall, white house happily ever after, and have walks to the park, ice-cream, pears, and lavender every day. "Please, please dear God, make things change..."

Morning: an air-bubble in Margaret's head and when she talked her throat was like the gardener raking the gravel drive. They called Doctor Cudlip, who was Nancy's father but much nicer than Nancy, and he said "Measles. Keep her warm in a dark room, and feed her only light food like steamed fish and rice pudding."

Margaret lay all morning in her tomb, except that it was hot, and instead of M. being free to fly around everywhere in a long white dress, scaring people like Nancy Cudlip, and Bruce, and Miss Pritchard, M. lay a prisoner in Margaret's body. And Margaret's body ached whichever way she turned; the bed got hotter and hotter, till the sheets were rumpled, and her nightgown as wet as a face-flannel.

All at once there were little red islands on her arms—on her chest, on her tummy; everywhere! The little red islands twitched, and she saw that they were the mounds of insects—biting and wriggling their way into her flesh till she wanted to tear them out as Nancy tore out Peter the lamb's eyes. Margaret was being eaten up alive!

"Miss Pritchard! Miss Pritchard, help! Oh, please come, Miss Pritchard!"

A fly buzzed round the bed. It wasn't a fly, it was a cockroach! The insects that were eating her were cockroaches!

"Help! Help! Oh, please help . . ."

"Now, Margaret, what on earth's this fuss?" Miss Pritchard with a tray. "I'm being eaten up by red cockroaches, please take them away, they're killing me, Miss Pritchard." "Don't be foolish, Margaret, or I'll be cross. Red cockroaches indeed, I never heard such nonsense!" "But Miss Pritchard, look!" "They're just the measle spots, that's all. You have to get rid of being ill by pushing out all the poisonous germs . . ." "I don't like them, please, take them off . . ." "Don't be so silly, Margaret, I *can't* take them off. You'll have to be a big girl and wait patiently till you're better. It won't be long, I promise you. Now sit up and eat some nice steamed fish and mashed potatoes, and after lunch I shall settle you down for a good rest . . ."

Margaret smelt of measles; the bed smelt of measles; everything smelt of measles; and poor M. was held a prisoner just like Daddy. P'raps it was one of the witch's spells!

What could she do?

Margaret played with her fingers, making birds and animals against the cracks of sunlight coming through the curtained windows, till she felt quite sick. Then she closed her eyes tight, pressing them with her knuckles to make beautiful patterns—stars, stripes like a galloping zebra, and great sheets of green fire.

She wanted to go to sleep for ever and ever, to be rid of her horrid, itchy body, her rabbit teeth and her cross-eyes, and to fly from it like a butterfly escaping from its wrinkled caterpillar-skin.

But dear God, she didn't want to die, she didn't mean sleep like that: not to go to sleep never to wake up—to be put into a coffin with the lid nailed down! To be buried in the dark!

Margaret couldn't breathe! Margaret's heart was going to stop beating! "Miss Pritchard! Miss Pritchard . . . please come quickly! Miss Pritchard!" "*Now*, what's the matter?" "I'm dying, Miss Pritchard." "Don't talk rubbish, Margaret, you're doing no such thing." "But I'm frightened of dying, Miss Pritchard." "Do stop being silly, Margaret, or I shall lose my temper. Why have you thrown off all your bedclothes? I've told you to keep properly covered up." "I couldn't *breathe*, Miss Pritchard." "Now, stop this nonsense *at* once and go to sleep." "Am I going to die, Miss Pritchard?" "Of course not—you don't die of the measles. What a curious child you are!" "But I will die one day, won't I?" "Of course—we all have to die one day. But dying is nothing to worry about: you just fall asleep and wake up in heaven, that's all. In any case, you don't have to think about it for a long time yet—you're only a little girl, and people only die when they get very old and sleepy." "Are you old, Miss Pritchard?" "No, I'm not. At least, not very old—I'm middle-aged." "Do you feel sleepy yet, Miss Pritchard?" "Not in the least! Now no more talking, please, and rest. I'll get you up at tea-time for a bit, and you can play with your toys in bed. If you're a good girl, I'll let you do a jigsaw puzzle . . ." "Will Mummy die soon, Miss Pritchard?" "No, Margaret, of course she won't—your mother's still a young woman." "Please, Miss Pritchard, read me a story." "No, Margaret, I haven't got time. I have to go to the village for your mother, and you have to sleep." "But I can't sleep—I'm not sleepy." "You must sleep to get well quickly. Now stop playing me up!—there, I'll tuck you in properly." "But I'm *boiling*." "The doctor says you must keep warm." "Does Daddy know I'm measled?" "Of course." "Why doesn't he come and see me?" "He's in London till the end of the week. I expect he'll come and see you when he gets back." "Will he see Gran in London?" "I expect so." "Why doesn't Gran come and see me?" "Because she's not very well." "Is it measles?" "Not exactly. Now that's quite enough. Go to sleep."

The door closed and Margaret was alone—except for M., of course. Nothing. Nothing for hours, and then only Miss Pritchard with tea, and after tea, a jigsaw puzzle. She *loathed* jigsaw puzzles—she always lost pieces in the bed. Pieces of jigsaw and breadcrumbs! She had prayed for a change, but this was much worse. There was no one to talk to—except M., of course, but now M. was imprisoned in Margaret's measly body. Oh, for a real friend...

> Ride a cock horse to Banbury Cross
> To see a fine lady upon...

A white horse—no, a pony—trotted up to the bedside. He loved Margaret, though he didn't usually like little girls. Margaret was different, because she was very clever and interesting, and was two people, Margaret and M. Margaret was ugly with braces, squint-eyes, and flat hair that just would not curl; and M. was as fair as a lily, invisible to everyone except Bradshaw. He was called *Bradshaw*, like the railway timetable in the hall. Bradshaw was a lovely name: it meant a train to London, a boat to India, or Peter Pan wings to the moon—to places where there was no Mummy, no Miss Pritchard, and no smell of measles; where instead, there was the smell of lavender, and children, hand-in-hand with their daddies, ran down sunflower yellow beaches to a sea as blue as forget-me-nots sparkling in the sunlight; and waves, cold as ice-cream, frothed along the sands . . .

Beautiful Bradshaw! Margaret stretched for the tin of talcum-powder on the pedestal cupboard and smelt it deep down. It was Bradshaw's breath.

Bradshaw talked a foreign language that only Margaret and M. could understand. Up to now he'd been very lonely because no one had been able to understand him. His daddy had gone away on a long journey, and his mummy couldn't be bothered with Bradshaw because he hated hunting. She was a thoroughbred who'd won a lot of prizes, but no one liked her because she kicked. What Bradshaw liked was going on long journeys by himself; but now there was Margaret and M. to keep him company it would be even better. He'd been lonely till now, but now he wouldn't be lonely any more.

"You see I hate other children and parties and so on. They always want to play musical chairs, or hide-and-seek, or guessing games, and I'm awfully bad at them." "So am I, Bradshaw, and the beastly grown-ups force you to join in, and they go on for simply ages."

The door opened to Miss Pritchard in brown overcoat and black hat—Margaret's heart jumped!

"Margaret—whom are you talking to?"

"No one, Miss Pritchard, I was just singing myself asleep."

"Very well, then. I'm off now—you be a good girl for two hours, and don't get out of bed for anything unless you have to go to the bathroom. I'll be back in two hours with some orange juice for you, but you won't get any unless you sleep! Good night."

The door closed and Miss Pritchard's steps died away. Bradshaw put his head out from under the pillow.

"I don't like her—I want to kick her." "She's not too bad sometimes, Bradshaw: the trouble is she's in league with the witch. We'll have to get rid of the witch because she's our mortal enemy, and holds Daddy in her power. Miss Pritchard's the witch's spy." "We must invent a special secret language, dear-heart, so that you and I can talk when she's about without her knowing." "Yes, Bradshaw, but how?" "You ask me a question by just thinking it, and I'll either shake or nod my head."

Margaret was convalescing. Hide-and-seek in the garden with Bradshaw; lovely fun, and very different from the hide-and-seek at children's parties where they pounced on you and scared you.

Long, perilous voyages to gather magic herbs to turn Mummy into a worm, and Miss Pritchard into a gorse bush. They didn't find it, but they would one day.

"You should send her to the sea-side for a while. She's a bit rundown, and after measles the sea air works wonders..."

Margate: The sun sparkling down on the sea. The beach was crowded with children with buckets and spades. Miss Pritchard, looking like a ferret in her black hat and brown overcoat, sat in a deck-chair knitting something long and purple.

"What's that you're knitting, Miss Pritchard?" "A muffler for my nephew." "The one who's at sea, Miss Pritchard?" "Yes, Margaret, now don't start pestering me with questions, there's a good girl. Run away and play. Why don't you build a sandcastle like the other children?"

Miss Pritchard put aside her purple knitting and took out a writing pad. "Miss Pritchard can go and eat *sea-weed*! Come along, dear-heart, I'll race you down to the water."

Margaret and Bradshaw tied, then they raced, splashing, just along the edge of the water.

Margaret and Bradshaw shrimping in the warm, shallow pools by a breakwater that was as green as spinach and smelt like kippers.

Margaret and Bradshaw digging huge, fortified castles for

them to take refuge in:

> Margaret's Queen of the Castle,
> Margaret's Queen of the Castle,
> Mummy's a dirty rascal!

Margaret and Bradshaw watching children having donkey rides, three breakwaters up the beach and back for sixpence. Margaret and Bradshaw chuckled with glee—wouldn't those children just be green with envy if they knew that Margaret Finlay had a white pony all to herself whenever she wanted it?

Margaret and Bradshaw swore to be friends in secret, to fight together and to voyage together, till death did them part.

V

Margaret Finlay's gas-fire flickered, turned blue, and died. Of course, it needed another shilling. She went to the tin box in the chest o' drawers where she kept silver for the gas, and copper for the telephone.

When the white clay bars were glowing again, she examined her water-colour, holding it from her at arm's length. Yes, it was finished, and rather good—though she said it herself "as shouldn't," as Gladys Peach would say.

But how odd! She'd meant to give a chestnut horse a background of green hills, and instead she had him before a sea as blue as the Mediterranean. The horse looked a wee bit out of place, actually, but he was full of life and his tail swished in the sea breeze. As a matter of fact, the painting was almost worth a frame—she could get one at Woolworth's, plain black, for half a crown.

With a great sense of satisfaction—a sense, almost of elation—she cleared up the mess, poured out her nightcap glass of milk, and took from the biscuit-tin two chocolate digestives—her favourites. If she was going to make that early start for Ely and avoid the London exodus, she had better hit the hay at once.

Chapter Three

I

As soon as Norma Gracewell came into the typists' room she began burbling about the smashin' time she'd been 'aving over Easter, and the t'riffic thing that had happened just when she'd thought she was in for a reely lousy 'oliday.

Gladys Peach, nursing a sensation of her own that was not going to be spoilt by anyone if she knew anything about the game, demanded somewhat peevishly of Norma, what. Nola Fleisch paused not an instant in the sorting of the office mail. Miss Finlay began a rigorous clean-out of her drawer.

Well, Norma had gone to a jam session at the Pallay with the gang, and a t'riffic'ly good-looking Yank, an absolute smasher, he was, a sergeant in the air force, had asked her for a dance and had been with her ever since—'cept to go to bed of course (and Norma gave Gladys Peach a wicked smirk). He'd even brought her to the office that very morning in his car, which was a smashin' Austin 'ealey, red and ever so fast; and he came from a place called— guess what?—Sandwich in Illinoyse. His name was Johnny Finkbine, and—guess what, Gladys?—he'd asked her to marry him, and what's more she'd accepted; so when she got 'ome last night she told Ma and Pa, and Pa had fair blown his top carrying on suthink dreadful till Ma shushed him. Now Pa was going to meet Johnny and talk to him; she was being called for by him that very night to take him 'ome to supper. And Johnny was going to ask Pa if he could marry her as quickly as possible, so for all she knew she would be Mrs Johnny Finkbine and a G.I. bride before the week was out—wasn't it a scream? She would be married before Gladys!

"Oh, no you won't," snarled Gladys, "it takes three weeks to publish the banns."

"Not if you're married in a registry office, so there!" Norma answered.

"Well, I've heard that Americans are fast workers, and now I know."

"All right, old puss-cat, I knew you'd be jealous."

Mr Bacon, sheaf of insurance invoices in hand, banged through the door. His face was gamboge, his eyelids magenta, and the jacket of his navy suit speckled with hair and dandruff. He looked as if he had just crossed the English Channel in a howling storm, in charge of three moulting red setters.

"Na then, lassies, did you all have a good Easter? Coom on, tell your Uncle Herbert all about it."

Poor Mr Bacon, he was making a valiant effort to be jovial in spite of his hangover.

"You've got to congratulate me, Mr Bacon," said Norma, "I'm going to be married to a Yank jet pilot, and poor old Glad is green as grass with jeal..."

"I'm not one bit jealous, Norma Gracewell, why should I be? You're not married yet, remember, and your American hasn't got permission from his C.O. yet—has he? So I shouldn't count my chickens before they're hatched if I was you."

"Johnny hasn't got to get permission from anyone, he's over twenty-one."

"That makes no difference. He *has* to get permission from his C.O.—all the boys do when they're overseas to stop them getting mixed up with the wrong sort of girl."

"How—how do they find out about the girl, whether she's the wrong sort or not," Norma faltered.

"Special investigators, I expect," Gladys triumphed. "I saw a film all about it. The C.O. put his foot down, and the boy was posted back to the States, and the girl killed herself. It was lovely."

"Why didn't she follow him to the States?" asked Norma strickenly.

"Really, Norma, I don't remember—I don't have films on the brain like some people I could mention, you know. Besides, what difference could it possibly make to you? I can't see you drowning yourself in the Thames over one boy. Easy come, easy go, as far as you're concerned."

Norma's eyes were watering, her lower lip was tremulous.

"Take no notice of her, lass," said Mr Bacon, "can't you see she's just kidding? Congratulations, ducks, I'll toast you and your lad in a pint, as soon as I'm able."

"It's quite true, Norm," said Gladys, repenting slightly now that she had vanquished her rival so completely; "I was only just teasing, that's all. Of course it's going to be all right with your American: congratulations from me, too. At least, I expect it'll work out all right eventually. You might have to wait a bit longer than a week, that's all."

"I also have to congratulate you, Norma," said Mrs Fleisch; "I wish you and your Johnny Finkbine much pleasure."

Miss Finlay mumbled something about best wishes and all that sort of rot, wound some letter heading into her machine, and began typing very fast. She had to get a letter off to Daddy in Bombay, before Mr Boothby rang his bell to summon her to dictation.

Dear Daddy: (she typed) . . .

"I've got some news, too," said Gladys. "It's all arranged that George and I get married in June. The wedding's going to be in

St Michael and All Angels, Ruislip, which is ever such a lovely church; and I'm going to have a dress made by a real French dressmaker who lives near us, and afterwards the reception's going to be at the Cumberland Hotel—Daddy won some money on the dogs yesterday, and he's promised. And George's father says he'll lend us the car to go to the South of France for our honeymoon."

"Cor..." breathed Gladys.

Miss Finlay's left hand knocked over the plastic dish of paper-clips, and she squatted, ungainly on her haunches, to pick them up off the floor. She was pedalling, pedalling, in high gear; she was pushing with all her weight on the pedals till her thighs ached; but still they gained on her, the monkey-screeching cycle club.

"But this is incredible," exclaimed Mrs Fleisch. "I, too, have some news. Rudi, my friend who has taken me to Maidenhead, wants me to marry him as soon as he is getting a divorce from his wife. Of course, I have accepted."

"Well caught!" screamed Norma, "Boothby's have scored the hat-trick! One more and they'd have to get a whole new typists' room."

They all looked at Miss Finlay who was picking up the last of the paper-clips—a few had fallen under the filing cabinet, which she could only get at from behind. She was conscious of the silence, of her own heavy breathing, and of her rump protruding solid as a hippopotamus's.

"Here, Miss Finlay," said Mr Bacon, "let me give you a hand with those."

"It's all right, thanks," she mumbled, continuing to conceal herself; then, recollecting her manners, she rose scarlet in the face, and regained her seat with what dignity she could muster. "I mean it's frightfully decent of you, but I've finished now—thanks awfully just the same. It was frightfully clumsy of me to spill them."

"How did you spend your Easter, Miss Finlay?" asked Mr Bacon gently. "Did you do summat interesting?"

He was being kind: at children's parties they'd said, "Never mind, Margaret dear, perhaps you'll be chosen first next time. Don't stand in the corner sulking, dear: you must learn to be a good sport—like your mother." A wave of anger rose inside her till she nearly choked.

"I cycled to Ely, if you want to know," she said, "with . . . Bradshaw!" She had meant to say "paint-box." She was a little astonished by her slip of the tongue.

"Bradshaw! Who's she?" asked Gladys, probably having in mind a games mistress called by her surname.

"Bradshaw, Miss Peach," said Miss Finlay in a voice that was as clear as a church bell, "has been my lover ever since I was eight."

This was an exaggeration, of course—she knew that very well—but she was utterly sick of these nattering peahens and their idiocies. If she was going to give them something to talk about, it might just as well be something worthwhile, and the consternation of their three vacuous faces was very enjoyable— very enjoyable indeed. Mrs Fleisch's astonishment had brought her letter-sorting to a complete stop. With her mouth opened and her eyebrows raised she had the look of a secretary-bird startled by a flying fish. Gladys and Norma were positively goggling, and even Mr Bacon with his hangover had turned from saffron to curry. Rats to their refugee jewellery manufacturers, weddings in white, and American airmen!—just for once she'd show them a thing or two, herself.

"What's Bradshaw's second name?" asked Norma, shrill with incredulity.

"Bradshaw," Miss Finlay answered promptly: "his first name is 'Pony'—it's short for Ponikwer Peter Aylestone Bradshaw—quite a collection of names, isn't it?"

That settled Norma—it was as plain on her face as a neon sign. No one could ever think up a name like Ponik-what? Fancy old Rabbit-face having a boy friend all this time and keeping him all to herself, too. She didn't expect they did much together except cycle; still it was a bit of a shock all the same.

Gladys Peach, however, was far from convinced.

"Miss Finlay, did you say he was your *lover*!"

"Why, yes, Miss Peach. We've been sweethearts ever since I had the measles. As a matter of fact, they got rather worried, and separated us by sending me to boarding school. Poor old Bradshaw had to go abroad, all by himself—to India as a matter of fact. But he's home again now, thank heavens."

"What's his job?" asked Gladys—her voice was dangerously soft: she was trying to trick Miss Finlay.

"I'm afraid he's a bit of a jack-of-all-trades. Up to now he's been too restless, too much of a wanderer, to get really settled, but perhaps he'll change his mind now he's come home. He's really a born globe-trotter: he's been to India—as I said—and Palestine, and China and Japan. Now he's just got back from North America."

"North America?" queried Mr Bacon, "which part? if you'll excuse me asking—I was there for a time during the war."

"Oh, Hollywood, actually."

"Hollywood!" exclaimed Norma, pop-eyed; "whatever was he doing there?"

"He was in films. He made two or three Westerns—you know, all that Cowboy and Indian rubbish—but the films were incredibly bad, and the poor dear so loathed making them, it just got him down. So now he's back with me in a temporary job—delivering milk, as a matter of fact. He says there isn't much glamour about it, but it is real."

"What's he look like?" asked Gladys. "Do you have any photos?"

"No, as a matter of fact—not with me, that is. But I've just done a water-colour of him that really isn't bad. I'd like to frame it and hang it, but he would just hate that: he's so terribly shy it just isn't true."

"Is he good-looking?" demanded Norma.

"Good heavens, no," said Miss Finlay, giggling at the idea, "not in the very least. Don't be deceived because he was in Hollywood into thinking him one of those film-star types. He's pleasant-looking, you know, but very ordinary: about six foot two; curly brown hair, brown eyes and very strong teeth. He's broad in the shoulder, but narrow in the hip. Every inch a thoroughbred, that I will say."

"Cor . . ." breathed Norma, using her technicolor imagination to the full. "And he gave up being a fillum-star to deliver milk! What a bloomin' ass!"

"Well, Norma," Miss Finlay answered, allowing herself a slight smile, and giving Mrs Fleisch a knowing nod, "there are other considerations, I suppose:—*Le cœur a ses raisons*, you know. But hark at me chattering away and not doing a stitch! Messrs Boothby and Gold will give me the sack, then I shall be entirely dependent on what old Bradshaw earns, which will land us both properly in the cart"—Miss Finlay burst into a nigh-uncontrollable fit of the giggles, but she managed to straighten her face just enough to continue. "As a matter of fact," she went on, "I rather want to leave early tonight—Bradshaw's sister and brother-in-law are dining with us. I suspect it's to give me the once-over, so I want to make sure of my cooking. Could I possibly ask you, Miss Peach, to take over any work that Mr Boothby may want after five o'clock?"

"I'm sorry, Miss Finlay, but tonight I can't possibly—I've

51

arranged to meet George, you see . . ."

"Please, Miss Finlay," broke in Mrs Fleisch, "this I will do with much pleasure, and it will be much pleasure, also, if you and Mr Bradshaw will come to me to Belsize Park for supper one evening, to meet my fiancée, Rudi Wertheim."

"Thank you so much, Mrs Fleisch, as soon as we're a little more settled we'd love to."

"Well, I'd best be getting summat done myself," said Mr Bacon in a voice curiously forlorn, and the door closed softly behind him. He reminded Miss Finlay a little of herself, though why, exactly, she was unable to determine. He probably felt like a small boy surrounded by giggling females, and rather out of things as a result.

Miss Finlay's typewriter began to clack energetically. It was such ages since she had last written to Daddy, and she had simply loads to tell him.

II

That evening she sped back home effortlessly, the traffic melting before her, the cool April air crossing her cheeks and fondling her hair, and the pedals spun beneath her feet as if of their own will. She was riding a flying horse, and horse and rider were as one: they swooped and soared through the crawling lines of traffic as swift as a seagull skimming the waves, and in her heart was a rare exultation.

When she landed at Ebury Street, she dismounted, and led her foam-flecked steed into his warm stable, grateful—as so often before—for his superb agility.

There was a creaking, a puffing and a wheezing on the stairs, and the wretched Mrs Twitcher, her landlady, appeared from her cabbage-smelling, subterranean cave.

"Just one moment if you please, Miss Finlay," she croaked, "I'm afraid I've 'ad more complaints about that bicycle of yours. Mr Morrish fell over it again last night—gave 'imself a nasty bruise on the shin, he did. I'm afraid I'll 'ave to ask you to leave it outside. Why don't you chain it to the railings so them kids won't be able to get at it?"

"I'm sorry, I can't possibly discuss it now, Mrs Twitcher—you'll have to excuse me for I'm late for an appointment. I'll come down later and see you."

She ran up the stairs two at a time, and in desperate haste unlocked her door. When she had it shut behind her, she turned the key and slid the bolt; then she leant against it, and stood motionless for a while in the gathering dusk, till her heart ceased to pound and her breathing grew steady. The yellow curtains sighed gently on the evening breeze; the Victoria traffic rumbled in the distance like a distant battle.

She went to her armchair and curled up in it, hugging her knees, her eyes tight shut.

"Bradshaw," she asked, "was I wrong to tell those chattering peahens about us? Have I betrayed your trust?"

"Dear-heart, of course not. You have never betrayed my trust."

"You never reproach me, Bradshaw, and I love you for it. My dear, I must get hold of a photo or something, for those ninnies at the office are incapable of understanding anything but the immediately obvious. What on earth can I do?"

"Go to a press agency, dear-heart, and find some Hollywood pin-up boy, and scrawl, 'To dearest Margaret, with love from Bradshaw.'"

"Bless you, Bradshaw dear, that'll satisfy their school-girl imaginations. Your ingenuity never fails. Oh, Bradshaw, I've missed you and missed you—where have you been all these years?

All this time you've been away, I've been like half a person—like a horse on two legs..."

The window exploded behind her. With a terrible shock she sprang to her feet and wheeled round to face her enemies. The lower pane of glass was a spider's web with a great hole at its centre. Boys were shouting in the street:

"Yer schewpid bleeder, Johnny, you'll 'ave the old woman after us now."

"You froo the ball, it was your fault."

"You swiped it, dincha? Come on, let's bugger off quick..."

"I know you boys, Johnny Flanagan, it's you—I saw you! I'll 'ave the police after you, I will! I'll tell your ma!" Mrs Twitcher was very, very angry. She would be shaking her fist, at least, or waving a broom handle in the air.

Miss Finlay stared at the web of cracked glass—it reminded her of the war. She was quivering all over with fright: she felt there was a tear in the hull of her submarine through which the seas would pour at any minute. She rushed to the light switch—In the hard, yellow light, her room was empty—as empty as the sick-room of the school san. when it was waiting for a patient. No torrent of foaming sea-water cascaded through the window: a battered black cricket ball lay on the grey rug, like a relic of the battle of Blenheim. "Those boys should be thrashed for their destructiveness. They were wicked, wicked, and one day they would be truly sorry..."

"Are you all right, Miss Finlay?" Mrs Twitcher was knocking.

"Yes, thank you, Mrs Twitcher."

"May I come in?"

"I'm just changing, Mrs Twitcher. I'll clean up the mess in a minute."

"I just want to see what damage them kids 'ave done, I won't worry you for more than a minute..."

"Could you possibly come up later, Mrs Twitcher? It's really not very convenient at the moment. I'll come downstairs when I'm ready—they've just broken one window, that's all."

Mrs Twitcher, grumbling, retreated down the squeaking stairs. Margaret Finlay's room was her own again, but it was empty of anything except misery, misery as flat, as cold, and as relentless as the rain of the Fens. She sank back in the armchair, shivering, and staring at the livid bars of the unlit gas-fire. And Black Thursday welled up within her uncontrollably like sea-sickness, till it enveloped her entirely . . .

III

A sunny afternoon in the garden—Margaret's ankles sliced through the fallen leaves like a great steamship cleaving through the ocean. M. and Bradshaw were on a most perilous quest: the king, M.'s father, was sick unto death, for he had been bitten by the Snake-woman, who had enmeshed him in her spell. Because of his illness a blight had overcome the land, causing all the leaves of the trees to wither, and the rich and fertile pastures to become desert.

The wise men had consulted the oracle, and had learnt that the remedy was a special flower found only on the loftiest mountains of the Himalayas. The only one in the kingdom who had any hope of finding this flower was the Princess M., the fairest, bravest and cleverest damsel in all the land. For this reason, the princess had equipped herself and her faithful companion for a long voyage. She disguised herself as a boy, since grave dangers beset innocent maidens who travel through wild and savage lands.

Princess M. and Bradshaw had crossed the stormy oceans; they had traversed three great forests, deep and dark; they had trailed across the Gobi desert that sweltered under a fiery sun. At long last, after much travail, and several hair-breadth escapes from robbers, wild beasts, and so on, they reached the sheer sides of the soaring Himalayas—the final and most terrible obstacle to their perilous mission.

"Bradshaw, I fear we will lose our lives on these treacherous rocks, for my strength is fast waning." "Fear not, dear-heart, hold on to my tail and we will yet reach the summit. Remember that the king your father's life—nay, more, the happiness of all the good people of this kingdom—depends on our success. So be of good courage, and we will yet triumph over the Snake-woman and all her evil works."

At long last, Princess M. and Bradshaw stood on the loftiest peak in the world, and there, at their feet, was a tiny clump of the tiny purple flowers that alone could rid the country of its blight.

"Before we pick it, Bradshaw, let's kneel and pray to God-the-Father-God-the-Son-and-God-the-Holy-Ghost, like us, three-in-one and one-in-three; for it is surely by His help alone that we have reached our goal." "Yes, but don't let's sing any psalms, dear-heart, they're so awfully long." "All right, we'll just kneel and pray, and I'll take off my clothes and offer myself as homage . . ."

Miss Pritchard's face at the nursery window.

"What are you doing on the rockery, Margaret?"—her voice was funny. "I was just playing Miss Pritchard." "Whom are you talking to?" "No one, Miss Pritchard." "Who's Bradshaw, then?" "Just a pony, that's all." "You'd better get down from there at once, before your mother catches you. You know very well she's forbidden you to play on the rockery. Why have you undone your dress?" "I was praying, Miss Pritchard—I mean I was so hot." "Do it up at once, and untuck your skirt from your bloomers. I don't want any more of this nonsense! What have I always told you about people who talk to themselves? Where do they go?" "I don't know, Miss Pritchard." "Yes, you do, Margaret, don't you fib to me; where do they go?" "To the lunatic asylum." "Right, Margaret, just you remember that."

Miss Pritchard thought she was going mad! Miss Pritchard, the spy, would tell Mummy! Hide Bradshaw quick; bury him in the darkest corner there is and cover him with shadows—the Snake-woman was a huntress who loved to trap animals so that her dogs could get their cruel teeth into their throats. M. knew all about Mummy's wickedness—she'd heard her tell stories of her huntings and killings till the dogs themselves had howled in fear. But Mummy was not going to destroy Bradshaw—not even if she set her dogs on to Margaret herself.

"Margaret, your mother wants to see you in the drawing-room." Miss Pritchard, spy and traitress, walked on to the lawn looking guilty. Now for it . . .

IV

Mummy was resting on the sofa, a tea tray on the low table by her side. She trickled smoke from her nostrils, holding the cigarette in an ivory holder; her white fingers were long and crimson-clawed.

"Come here, Margaret . . . Margaret, I said come here! Don't stand cowering at me: when I tell you to do something, do it at once . . . Why do you look at me like that? I'm not going to eat you! And for goodness' sake stop flinching like that before I've even touched you. I don't want a daughter that's a coward, you know—one in the family is quite enough. If you've done anything wrong, own up." "I haven't done anything wrong." "Oh, yes you have, don't you lie to me. You were on the rockery, weren't you, when I've told you, and Miss Pritchard's told you, that you are not to. I will not have my flowers trampled on by your big feet. Now come here and sit down—I told you to stop cringing every time I move my hand; I'm not going to hit you! What a gutless little creature you are! What's all this about your talking to a horse, or something?"

A sudden movement of Margaret's right elbow knocked over the silver milk jug. It soaked the fingers of toast on their lace doily, and splashed black measles on Mummy's blue silk dress—islands spreading on a shimmering sea.

"You dirty little tike, I believe you did that on purpose." "I didn't do it on purpose, I'm sorry." "I've a damn good mind to tell your father to give you a thrashing when he gets home—except that he'd probably faint at the very idea. Well, I shall give you a good hiding myself, do you hear me if you don't tell me the truth at once. What is this nonsense about a horse?" "I don't know." "You're lying, and I shall tan your hide for you. Miss Pritchard told me not five minutes ago that you were climbing over the rockery half undressed, babbling to yourself like an idiot, and that when she asked you what you were doing you told her you were talking to a horse." "I was playing a game." "What was the horse called?" "I don't know." "You're lying again, Miss Pritchard told me you called it 'Bradshaw'. Is that true?" "No." "Then Miss Pritchard was lying." "No." "Well, then, if she wasn't lying, you are." "I don't know." "Oh, yes, you do, don't you?"

The hand holding her wrist was soft and cool. The sharp nails touched the inside flesh for a moment, while the green snake-eyes searched into the secrets of her cave. Then Mummy laughed, soft, poisonous laughter.

"All right, my poppet, have it your own way. What you need is the company of decent, normal, healthy girls—girls of your own age who'll knock this nonsense out of you."

V

Margaret, in bed, could hear Mummy talking to Daddy in the drawing-room down below, and M. knew they were talking about her, Margaret, and Bradshaw.

"Get out of bed, Margaret, and listen through the floorboards." "It's better in the corner by the pipes—Mummy sounds as if she's at the bottom of a well..."

"I didn't know she had it in her—I'm glad she has anything at all!—poor little thing is so plain-takes after your family, Gordon, not mine—always snivelling and sulking..."

Daddy mumbled—he was deeper in the well than Mummy, and M. couldn't hear him very well.

"I didn't say she wasn't!"—Mummy again. "The fact remains this nonsense must be stopped—there's enough queerness in the family without encouraging more—Miss Pritchard's an old sheep. Margaret needs boarding-school and that's flat—can't be more expensive than paying and feeding a governess!"

Silence. Daddy was hiding behind his paper. Margaret, shivering, crawled back into bed. The sheets were still warm, but her feet were cold as linoleum.

"So, Margaret, my dear, they're sending us to boarding-school! Well, it can't be worse than parties, can it and at least you won't have to walk to the village any more with Miss Pritchard." "No, M., and we have got Bradshaw, haven't we? Bradshaw, you can come out of hiding now." "Is the coast clear?" "Yes, Bradshaw. They're sending us on a real journey now, to boarding-school. It'll be fun, won't it and they won't really be able to hurt us while we have each other, will they? And we'll never let them take us away from each other, will we?" "Never, dear-heart, never, never, never"—Bradshaw's voice soared like the church choir descant.

"Good night, Bradshaw." "Good night, dear-heart, God bless

you."

Bradshaw wrapped his four legs round Margaret to keep her warm, and he hummed to her "Ride-a-cock-horse" to send her to sleep.

VI

Margaret in the train, on her way to London. Opposite was Mummy in a fur coat with a high fox collar over her shoulders. She was wearing a black dress, and she read a big magazine about clothes. Margaret was wearing her best grey flannel skirt and jacket, and a hat with a brim. Margaret, M., and Bradshaw looked out of the window at fields and back gardens whirling past, and the train smoke cotton-woolling into nothingness.

"Dear-heart, will Mummy take us to Gran's?" "I don't know, Bradshaw. It's better not to ask in case that makes her say No. Guess, and see if you're right." "I don't want to guess. Look at that lady eating toffees—she's dribbling at the corners of her mouth, and that's her fourth at least. She's a greedy old lady—Miss Pritchard would have something to say to her about that!" "Yes, Bradshaw, she'd say that it was rude to stare!"

London. The train jerked and hissed to a stop. The station was huge and smelt of fish and soot. People standing still like cows in a field; people running hither and thither like hens. A porter with a barrow piled with cases was chased by a woman with a worried face and two children, one on each arm.

"Come along, Margaret, don't dawdle."

Inside a taxi: it was dark like the inside of a box of chocolates, but it smelt of petrol and leather. A nice smell, much nicer than Mummy's perfume. Margaret knelt on the shiny seat and stared out of the tiny quivering window in the back: Princess M. was driving secretly through her capital, for no one was to know she was there.

Harrods. They thought it was a shop, but it was really Princess M.'s palace.

"The schoolgirls' clothing department, please?" "Straight through the main hall, and on the left, Madam."

A thin, little lady with a humped back, gold spectacles pinching her nose spitefully. Her nose was very long, and pink at the tip.

"Can I help you, Madam?"

"I'm Mrs Finlay. I telephoned yesterday and spoke to a Miss Dullard about the St Faith's uniform for my young daughter." "I'm Miss Dullard, Mrs Finlay; will you come this way, if you please— you *and* the young lady."

Miss Dullard had very big ears, and hair pulled into a bun stuck with more hairpins than Margaret had ever seen on one head. Miss Dullard shed them as she walked and Margaret picked up three to take home.

Mummy ordered lots and lots of clothes, more clothes than Margaret had ever had. New woolly underwear; pyjamas, pink and blue; navy tunic, navy knickers with elastic legs; black stockings; several white blouses; blue and gold tie; black hat with brim, all velvety like mole's skin; white straw hat with blue and gold bands; black shoes with laces; hockey boots, with great toecaps, and studs; two pairs of white gloves.

"You're a princess, dear-heart. You need the white gloves for shaking people's hands, so that your own don't have to touch them." "I don't like the hockey boots. I'm sure it's a horrid game, and I'll be bad, and they'll all hate me and kick me." "Then, you can spring on to my back, dear-heart, and we'll gallop away. Don't worry, you don't have to have anything to do with them while I'm there. Besides, you're a princess. Princess Margaret de Himalayas, and you can order them all to be put in dungeons if you like..."

"Margaret, do stop dreaming—thank you so much, Miss Dullard, you'll have that sent, then, and charged to my husband's account. Come along, Margaret, now we have to do a little shopping for me."

Another hall of the palace. The smell of perfume. Mummy bought a tiny bottle of *Fleur d'amour*, which meant flower of love: it smelt of sweetness, and dying flowers, and doctors.

Mummy bought a little flowered purse with a gold clasp, long black gloves, and stockings like grey smoke.

"Please charge it to my husband's account—Major Finlay, Aylestone Hall, North Essex." "Certainly, Madam, sign here if you please..."

"Bradshaw, will I be able to buy things by signing Daddy's name?" "No, dear-heart, you can only do that when you're Daddy's wife." "Will you let me sign your name for things, Bradshaw?" "Of course, dear-heart, when I've made some money." "How will you make money, Bradshaw?" "I'll search for gold..."

"Come along, please, Margaret, we'll have lunch here, I think. Afterwards we have to go and visit Grannie Finlay—I promised your father..."

"Bradshaw, did you hear?" "Yes, dear-heart, isn't it lovely! I guessed we would, but I didn't want to say in case you were disappointed." "Bradshaw, won't Gran get excited when I tell her about you!" "Yes, but don't tell her about the quest for the purple flower, 'cos grown-ups don't understand..."

"Margaret, sit down properly like a big girl. Here's the menu—what do you want to eat? Choose quickly, or I shall choose for you."

A tall, tall man with nasty black moustaches and cheeks as pink as ham was standing over the table.

"Celia, you didn't tell me you were coming to town..."

Mummy looked funny—naughty.

"*Prend garde, chéri, je suis avec l'enfant*—Margaret, this is Captain Hillyard, an old friend of Daddy's from India. Bunny, this is my daughter, Margaret."

"Hallo, Margaret."

"Hallo."

He talked with tapioca pudding sliming down his throat. His lips were wet.

"Margaret, say Good afternoon properly to Captain Hillyard."

"Good afternoon, Captain Hillyard."

"I don't think you need be so formal Margaret: why don't you call me Uncle Bunny?"

"Thank you."

He looked at Mummy as if she was an ice-cream and his mouth was watering.

"*Elle n'est pas* jolly *comme sa mère mais ça* is not surprising. *Vous étés certaine qu'elle ne comprong pas?*'

"Quite certain, Bunny, the wretched governess who's teaching her knows nothing herself. That's one of the reasons we've decided to send her to boarding-school. Margaret, Captain Hillyard just paid you a compliment in French—he said that you're a very nicely behaved little girl."

"She's lying, dear-heart. He said that you weren't pretty like Mummy. I don't like him." "Nor do I, Bradshaw . . ."

"Margaret, answer properly, and don't stare at the tablecloth when people talk to you—we're a bit shy, Uncle Bunny, that's the trouble. *Elle est très gauche, tout-à-fait comme sa père, malheureusment.* Yes, Uncle Bunny, Margaret's going to boarding-school next week."

"Jolly good show, Margaret, I expect you'll have bags of fun—hockey, netball, and all that sort of thing, eh? *Celia, pouvez-vous me voir cet aprés-midi? Je suis* absolutely mad for you . . ."

"*Prend garde, n'est ce pas!* Margaret and I have to go to Margaret's Grannie, Uncle Bunny, or we would love to accept your invitation, wouldn't we, Margaret"

"Celia, *je dois* talk, *c'est très important, je vous assure.* Take the child and leave her, and collect her later."

"Margaret dear, Captain Hillyard wants to talk over some business with me this afternoon. I'll take you to Grannie's and I'll leave you there—she wants to see you, not me, after all. I'll collect you at five for us to catch the train home . . ."

"Bradshaw, the whole afternoon with Gran to ourselves—isn't that beautiful? And Gran always has chocolate biscuits for tea."

VII

Gran in bed. A starchy nurse rustled about the darkened room tidying things—just like Miss Pritchard when Margaret had the measles. Gran a gnome, shrunken and wrinkled, her hands like the claws of dead chickens clenched on the coverlet, her mouth caved in till her nose and chin nearly met, her eyes milky as marbles.

"Nursh—nursh! My teef!"

"Here we are, Mrs Finlay, we thought you would brighten up when your little granddaughter arrived—didn't we?"

In a tumbler of water on the bedside table grinned enormous white teeth, the gums the colour of skinned rabbit. Nurse fished them out and handed them to the gnome; the gnome fumbled them to her mouth, sucked them horridly into place—and became Gran. And Gran gave Margaret a gentle smile.

"Dear-heart, coming to see your old bag o' bones Gran. Don't be afraid, dear—it's still me. Will you give me a kiss?"

Margaret touched the soft, wrinkled cheek with her lips and

smelt lavender—the old smell!—but when Gran sighed there was a new smell—a horrid smell, the smell of dung!

"Are you ill, Gran? Is it measles?" "No, dear, it's not measles exactly. Don't worry, I'll be as right as rain soon, then you can come to London and stay with me—would you like that?" "I'd love that, Gran, and we can go to the park and eat ice-cream. Are there chocolate biscuits for tea, Gran? Oh, I've missed you and missed you. Why didn't you come to see me? I hated it till Bradshaw came." "Bradshaw? Who's Bradshaw?" "Bradshaw's a pony who plays with me. He talks to me, and goes on long, perilous journeys with me. He loves you, Gran, because whenever he's pleased he wags his head up and down, and now he's wagging his head up and down like anything. But he hates Miss Pritchard—he wants to kick her—and he hates . . ." "Whom does he hate, dear? He ought not to hate anyone, you know—that's wicked." "Oh, he doesn't hate anyone really—except when people try and kill him. That's why they're sending me to school, Gran—they want to knock all the nonsense out of me. They think Bradshaw's nonsense. You don't think Bradshaw's nonsense—do you, Gran?" "Certainly not, dear-heart. I could tell them a thing or two that they'd think very great nonsense indeed, and they would be fools for thinking so, let me tell you. Whilst I've been lying here these past few weeks, do you know whom I've been seeing?—your daddy when he was a little boy not much older than you. 'Gordon,' I say to him, 'Gordon: you've gone and ruined your best jacket. Your father will be livid with rage when he sees it. You'd better run upstairs and change, and bring it to me to mend quickly—that woman would never mend it for you. Gordon, I tell you she's a greedy slut. You're a grown man, but you haven't the sense of a child. Can't you see through the mask, Gordon? Can't you see that she's one remove from the streets? She doesn't love you, I tell you. She loves your money and position! All right, marry her. No one can accuse me of being a possessive mother, and standing in my son's way; but I tell you that as sure as your name is Gordon Finlay, you'll rue the day you marry her, for the rest of your life! She hates me, I tell you, and she despises you. She's a wicked woman, a harlot!'"

Gran's eyes were watering, her feeble hands fluttering. Nurse bustled into the room and pushed between Margaret and the bed.

"It's all right, dear, it's all right, Mrs Finlay. You're just dreaming again, dear—there's no one here but your litttle granddaughter."

Gran looked round the room, tears on her cheeks.

"Oh, yes, of course, it's Margaret. I'm sorry, dear-heart, for a while I thought you were your father. And now you're going off to school, they tell me—everyone grows up so fast these days. Well, dear, don't forget me, will you; and come and see me in the holidays, and bring Daddy with you—if that woman will let him off her leash. She's a slut! I told him when he married her, but he would never listen. He would never listen . . . Kiss your Grannie on the cheek and say Good-bye, dear. Grannie's tired and wants to sleep now."

"Good-bye, Gran"—the lips moved and the claws tightened—"God bless you."

VIII

"Miss Pritchard—is Mummy a harlot?" "Margaret, don't you dare use such a word again! I've a very good mind to tell your mother." "But I only wanted to know what a . . ." "That's quite sufficient, Margaret." "Miss Pritchard, what does *sherry* mean in French? Is it a rude word, Miss Pritchard?" "Don't chatter so, Margaret, and concentrate on what you're doing. Untie those laces *properly—*

you know you won't have anyone to stand over you at boarding-school! You'll just get punished quick-sharp." "But is *sherry* a rude word, Miss Pritchard?" "Of course it isn't—it means 'darling' that's all. Now hurry into bed, quick-sharp, and I'll bring you your hot milk."

IX

Margaret in her new long stockings; Margaret in her new navy blue tunic; Margaret in her new white blouse with the collar buttoned, and her new blue and gold tie tied in a knot just like Daddy's. The car drove off. Margaret waved at Miss Pritchard through the back window—Miss Pritchard waved a clean white hanky, and suddenly screwed up her face.

"Bradshaw, Miss Pritchard's crying!" "Yes, she is." "Why is she?" "P'raps because she's unhappy." "Why's she unhappy when she's going on a journey?" "P'raps because she hasn't anywhere to go." "But she's got her nephew, and ever so many people that she writes letters to—she's always writing letters, or knitting them mufflers." "P'raps they don't want Miss Pritchard's letters or her mufflers, dear-heart—you never wanted the hot milk, did you?"

X

They were saying good-bye in the Headmistress's study. The room was big and white, and there was a green carpet, and more books than Margaret had ever seen in her life, and a big desk covered with papers, and there was a clock in a red leather box. On the one wall which wasn't a bookcase there were lots of framed photos of girls in teams—they all wore tunics and white blouses like

Margaret's. The clock ticked away very quietly, but M., and Bradshaw could hear it quite clearly.

"Good-bye, old girl," Daddy said; but he didn't look at her—he just stared at the carpet. "Have a good time," he said. He pulled her towards him and she smelt his smell of tobacco and hair lotion; his moustaches tickled her cheek, and in her thoat there was a great lump of porridge.

"Good-bye, darling," Mummy sang, sweet as honey; "if you're a good girl we'll come and see you at half-term." She made a kissing noise in the air, two inches away from Margaret's face.

Margaret was *not* going to cry in front of *her*, and that was flat: she wouldn't, she wouldn't, she wouldn't.

"Write to us every now and then," said Daddy. "The girls write home every Sunday," said the Headmistress.

XI

The Headmistress was as tall as the grandfather clock in the hall at home. The red leather box on her desk went tick-tock quietly and her voice, too, went tick-tock quietly; but she frightened M., for it was as if someone was tapping on a window-pane with a hammer, one, two; three, four; five, six; seven, eight: if she wasn't careful the glass would . . .

"I know all about Bradshaw, Margaret, because your mother has told me. Now, it's all right for little girls who haven't many friends to play with to play make-believe with a pony; but you're not a little girl any more, are you, Margaret?—you're a big girl now! Besides, here at St Faith's there are lots of girls for you to play with, and you're going to make lots of friends, aren't you, Margaret? You can forget all about make-believe ponies now, can't you, Margaret? Can't you Margaret?"

"Bradshaw is *not* make-believe—Bradshaw will just show you how make-believe he is by giving you a jolly good kick! Bradshaw, you are real, aren't you? Whisper to me, Bradshaw, or nod to me, and tell me where you're hiding—oh, Bradshaw, please, please come quick so that I can leap on your back and have you carry me away..."

"Margaret, listen to me—d'you hear me? Margaret, stop day-dreaming at once..."

"Bradshaw, oh dear-heart Bradshaw, you promised me! You promised! Don't be afraid of her, Bradshaw, she can't hurt you..."

"Margaret, if you don't pay attention I shall have to cane you. Have you ever been caned on the hand? It's very painful, and I should hate to do it your first day. It's a great disgrace, too..."

"I'm not afraid of you, you old wardrobe, you. You could topple down and squash me flat for all I care. You can't hurt me—can she, Bradshaw? Bradshaw, can she?"

"... Bradshaw is a lot of nonsense. It's just a day-dream you made into a game, that's all. You know very well it's just a game—like dressing up in old clothes as something, or putting on nurse's uniform and playing hospitals. You must grow up, Margaret, you can't live in a dream all your life..."

The tapping on Margaret's poor forehead fell harder and harder, till her forehead cracked like a coconut, and her brains started to leak...

M. watched the spit at the corners of the Headmistress's mouth: it was like clusters of white bubbles floating on the waves. The Headmistress had hairs on her upper lip like a gooseberry, and yellow teeth like a great cart-horse. Bradshaw was hidden deep, deep in the deepest shadows of the cave. One day he would come out of his hiding-place and M. would climb on his back, and together they would go for a long, long, journey to a place where no one would ever trouble them again.

XII

A funeral. The poor flattened body of M.'s boon companion, covered with black velvet, was being carried on a stretcher to its last resting-place—the soldier's tomb in Princess Margaret's own chapel. Dear-heart Bradshaw mustn't lie in cold earth, with all that weight pressing down on his eyes and nostrils—that would be horrible!

The stretcher was put down on the tombstone. Princess M. took off her funeral robes to cover up Dear-heart and keep him warm; then she lay down by his side, her hands pressed together in prayer, like the crusader's wife in Aylestone church...

"Good gracious, child, what are you doing with no clothes on?" "Oh!" A woman in white—Gran's nurse! "I was praying, nurse." "Call me Matron, child—don't you remember me? I unpacked your trunk this afternoon!" "Yes, Matron." "Now, why have you taken off your pyjamas?" "Please, Matron, I was boiling hot." "Well, put them on again, and keep them on, or I shall have to report you to the Headmistress. If you're hot you can take off one of your blankets—here, I'll take it with me. Now, go to sleep. Good night." "Good night, Matron."

Margaret shivered under the thin blanket and cotton bedspread. The lump in her throat swelled and swelled till it burst—and Bradshaw? a little girl's game like making animals on the wall with your hands, a shadow that couldn't even keep her warm. Margaret was all alone.

XIII

Margaret Finlay was as cold and weak as if she had been violently sick. She opened her eyes: under the glare of the ceiling light the room was quite empty. This, then, was the reality. Much as she had hated the Head, the Head was really quite right. It was dangerous to let the imagination run riot. Telling little stories in the typists' room because she was bored was one thing, but allowing herself to play-act them when she was by herself was quite another. She was a big girl now—five weeks short of thirty-one—and she musn't play games with Bradshaw any more. If she was lonely, she must take pains to be less lonely, and make an effort to meet people again.

She could take another course at the Regent Street Poly—sculpture would be fun, or wood-carving. She would meet people that way. She could make a special effort to get on better with people at the office—not just studying them as if they were butterflies and she a collector, but getting to know them. One or two of them must be nice!—Mrs Fleisch for instance. She had been really very kind, inviting Margaret and Bradshaw to dinner. They could invite her to them, and Margaret could explain that Bradshaw was just a joke. Mrs Fleisch would understand . . .

Margaret Finlay sighed. She looked at her sensible watch—Heavens, it was ten thirty-three! No wonder she felt weak! What should she have to eat? This was late supper with a vengeance! She had better have something light: an omelet of three eggs, some bacon, a fried tomato, lots of toast and butter, some of the stewed prunes, and a mug of nice, soothing, hot chocolate—that just about filled the bill. And for company, the radio—some music.

As Margaret Finlay whisked the eggs, smelling the good butter browning in the pan, her feet irresistibly shuffled and tapped to the rhythm—Heavens! what *wouldn't* she do next? Why, she was *dancing*!

Chapter Four

I

On Miss Finlay's desk next morning there was a typed envelope addressed to her. Puzzled, she tore it open—it was a typed note on Boothby's small-sized letter-heading.

Dear Miss Finlay (she read):
May I take the liberty of asking your advice? I'm considering buying a bicycle and since I have admired your Raleigh for a long time, I am considering buying one of the same make. If you would be so kind as to give me some information about your model, I should be grateful. Might you spare the time to take lunch with me today, at any time convenient to you? If today does not suit you, could you manage it any other day this week? After an official acquaintance of more than eight years, I trust you will not find my request presumptuous. Please do not take offence.
The letter was signed, "*Yours sincerely, Herbert Bacon.*"

Strangely enough, Miss Finlay was not entirely surprised, though she felt that she ought to have been. Nevertheless, her heart began to pound with nervous apprehension as she re-read the letter—it was as if she had to make a speech in front of the class, or sing solo in the school concert. Her first reaction was to refuse Mr Bacon's invitation, or ignore it altogether. But she could hardly be so rude to someone she had known for eight years, who had never been anything but polite. Besides, hadn't she only last night resolved to try mixing more with people?

Lunch with Mr Bacon—an invitation from a gentleman. She must not be clumsy. Just for once, could she not be reasonably *femme-du-monde*?

She was sweeping into the already crowded restaurant, wearing an absurdly frivolous black velvet hat, whose veil gave her thickly-lashed eyes a mystery, a subtlety, that fascinated and bewildered men wherever she went. She sat at the table the obsequious *maître d'hôtel* bowed them to, and, with her lovely oval face tip-tilted intriguingly on tapering fingers in black gloves, she distilled a magic, at once fragrant and exotic, that made her escort's nostrils twitch, and his eyes dilate with desire. "Who is that fascinating woman?" every man in the restaurant asked, and all the women looked at her with envy and the inner conviction that compared with so elegant a figure, they looked like charwomen.

"My dear man," Margherita said in a voice husky but beautifully modulated; "you can't mean to start pedalling around London on a bicycle at your age! I mean, seriously, darling, don't *you* think it would be just a wee bit absurd." Her escort's face flushed with embarrassment, and she thrust her stiletto home with a careless wave of a slim wrist: "Darling, please don't be coy with me. You know, and I know, and you know I know, and I know you know I know, that I have been perfectly well aware of your—shall we say *penchant*—for me for some time, and it offends me not at all. As a matter of fact, my dear, I'm charmed and amused by it, and just a wee bit touched. I'm so sorry, so very sorry, that I can't marry you." She fitted a Turkish cigarette into an ivory holder, paused while he lit it with his monogrammed gold lighter, and inhaled deeply, luxuriously. "I can't marry you since I am already involved with another; but there is no reason why we should not be the best of friends. Only, my dear"—she laid her fingers for a fraction of a second on his sleeve—"let's have no pretence between us such as a bicycle. That would be unworthy." Mr Bacon stared at her, mouth agape. She blew over him a cloud of blue smoke, rich as incense...

No, no, the picture was absolutely wrong for Margaret—Margaret, don't-be-so-clumsy, of the largest feet in St Faith's. They would go to Lyons' in Fenchurch Street and queue up with a tray at the self-service. "What'll you have, lass?" "Can I have anything? I mean simply *any*thing?" Margaret in a navy gym tunic, white blouse, and black stockings. "Yes, lass, this is your treat. And call me Uncle Bert, will you?" "Thanks very much, Uncle Bert. May I have tomato soup and fried fish and chips; then two fried eggs, sausage and tomato; then meat pie, mashed potatoes and baked beans; and to follow, *Lyons' extra large strawberry-parfait*? Oh, gosh, I'm frightfully sorry!" In her excitement she'd grabbed hold of a water jug and upturned it, drenching him...

II

A short while later, a surprisingly calm and collected Margaret Finlay read her reply to Mr Bacon with some satisfaction.

Dear Mr Bacon (she had typed):
Thank you very much for your kind invitation to lunch. I shall be delighted to tell you all I can of my Raleigh *sports-roadster (as I think they list it in the catalogue). Today would do very well, and I would suggest one o'clock as a convenient time. The only condition I must insist on is that you allow me to pay for myself. Where shall I meet you?*
Sincerely,
M. Finlay

She folded the note, slid it into an envelope, and placed it immediately inside the insurance invoice folder, which she carried over to Mr Bacon without the least sign of confusion. He took the file eagerly, giving her a look that she tried to answer with a bright smile, which made her feel just like Gran's nurse. Mr Bacon, it was true, was a little gauche, a little absurd, for a man of his age.

But when he returned the folder, giving her just a suspicion of a conspiratorial wink, she felt apprehensive; and when she read:

Thanks very much. One o'clock, then, by your bike.
H. A. B.,

terror exploded in her tummy! She should never have accepted! What would they talk about? He was a horrid little man with beery breath! She hated talking and eating at the same time—she would so much rather read a magazine over a quiet meal all by herself. People were horrid. This was the very last time she would accept an invitation to lunch, she promised herself. It was worse than going to a children's party.

III

He was standing by her bike—she wasn't late; in fact, she was half a minute early.

"D'you want to examine it, Mr Bacon?"

He grinned: "I don't think so, thanks—I have examined it pretty thoroughly already, to tell you the truth."

"Would you like to have a go on it? I'll unlock it and you can try it out round the block."

"Thanks very much, I won't bother doing that. I'll lift it up instead to feel the weight."

"It's not a racing bike or anything like that, I'm afraid. I bought it for lots of hard wear—I like things to be solid."

"I quite agree. What would you want with a light, racing bike with all the town work you do? Shall we go and have a bite to eat? I know a nice little pub—if you've no objection."

"No, no, of course not." His Yorkshire accent was always more pronounced when he talked to her than when he talked to the others. Funny . . .

"It is mostly town work you do—on your bike, I mean." He took very large strides for a little man. Lord, he was going to take her arm crossing the street! No, he wasn't—thank Heavens.

"Well, I do a good deal of riding in town, of course, but on holidays and week-ends I cycle out into the country."

"Where d'you go eggs-actly?"

"Well, all sorts of places, really. I mean I go for old churches, or cathedrals—places like that."

"That's very inter-resting, Miss Finlay. Why d'you go to old churches?"

"Well, I like sketching rather, you see—buildings and old tombs, and so on."

"That's very inter-resting—here's the pub by the way: we'll go upstairs—the waitress knows me, you see."

A crowded dining-room—the smell of beef and cabbage, beer and tobacco. Red-faced men at small tables covered with white cloths. Brown Windsor or Mulligatawny soup for a cert: sort of boarding-school dinner. Let him order. *Do* sit down for once without spilling anything.

"Let's sit here, shall we? I don't know what you fancy, but I can recommend the steak-and-kidney pudding."

"That would be topping."

"Right, Lilly-luv, tomato soup, steak-and-kidney twice, and

bring us plenty of veg."

"Right-eeo, dear. Here's some rolls and butter to be getting on with." He probably knew all the waitresses by their first names—a man of the world!

"She knows I get hungry while I'm waiting, Miss Finlay. Here, have a roll. You were telling me about your sketching! Point of fact, I used to do some when I was in the navy—ships, mostly. Why do you do tombs? Isn't that a bit morbid?"

"Not at all. Tombs are so quiet and still, you know. They give you a lovely feeling of peace—besides, they're easy to draw."

"I know what you mean about the peace and quiet. I miss that in London, you know. Everyone is always rushing off somewhere to do something, as if they're never comfortable being where they are. When I was a kid, things were different. Oh, we lived in Huddersfield, my mother and me, and that's as dirty a town as ever I've set eyes on. But you stayed put more than in London. You got to know your neighbours, and you collected a friend or two who mattered. I've been in London eight years, I've changed digs eleven times, and I've met scores of people; and not one of them matter a toopenny damn one way or t'other. I meet them in the evenings for a pint, or I watch soccer with them week-ends, and there's an end of it. We know nowt about each other, and don't care to find anything out—that's how it is. It was different when I was in the navy: you got to know people then, because you lived with them. And it was different when I was a lad back in the North: there was a gang of us from the same school, and we'd play street cricket or street soccer, and we were in the scouts and visit castles, maybe, or an old church or two. Point of fact—by goom, you've reminded me!—we used to do brass-rubbings, and all that. But hark at me, nattering away. I talk too much, that's what. Have a roll and butter, Miss Finlay."

"I've always wanted to do brass-rubbings, but I've never

known how to. Do tell me, Mr Bacon."

"Well, you get your roll of paper, and you have the solution, and you coat the paper first..."

"What exactly is the solution?"

"Well, it's a sort of ammonia, I s'pose—you get it in art shops and places like that. But look here, Miss Finlay: why don't we go brass-rubbing together one Saturday afternoon. It's much easier to show you than to explain. I was never much at giving directions. Will you come with me?"

"I'd like to, Mr Bacon."

"How about this Saturday afternoon? We could go to St Albans—I bet they've got some lovely brass there!"

"Well, I don't really know about this Saturday..."

"Are you doing something else?"

"Well, not really—except, that I usually clean my room on a Saturday, and take my washing to the launderette, and that sort of thing."

"Why don't you do all that in the morning, and leave the afternoon free to go to St Albans with me? We could go round the cathedral, and then have tea."

It was a plot, of course. He was a sex-maniac, and he wanted to get her alone. Or the office had set him on to ask her out for a bet...

"Do say yes, Miss Finlay. I don't suppose I'll have my bike by then, but we could always go by Greenline bus—that is, if you don't ob-ject to the bus. Do you?"

"No. No, I don't object to the bus..."

"Then do say yes. We'd have such fun!"

"I... I don't really know what to say, Mr Bacon."

"Then say yes. Look, here's our lunch. Well done, Lilly-luv, you only took half an hour today!—don't mind me, Miss Finlay, Lilly and I always kid each other a bit, don't we, Lilly-luv?"

"'Course we do, ducks. Are you and the lady going to 'ave something to drink, dear, or will it be just coffee?"

"Would you like a glass of beer, Miss Finlay—no! All right, Lilly-luv, just make it two cups of coffee. Tomato soup, Miss Finlay. *Heinz.* Not as good as home-made, but not too bad. I hope you like food—I'm a pretty good trencherman myself. Point of fact, I do for myself in my digs—I've got a baby Belling cooker."

"What an extraordinary coincidence! So have I."

"D'you like cooking?"

"I love it."

"Good, we must compare recipes! P'raps we will on the bus on Saturday—you will come to St Albans with me, won't you?"

"All right. Yes, all right, I will, Mr Bacon."

IV

How strange it was getting to know people! Margaret wanted to, and didn't want to. She looked forward to the outing as if it was going to be a special treat, and she lay awake at night, staring at the shadows on the ceiling by the street lamp, and dreading it. The headlights of a passing car suddenly turned the room upside-down into a chamber of horrors! He was trying to trick her. He was going to find about Bradshaw so that he could tell all the office—it was all a ghastly joke! He was a murderer! He was going to take her to some dark corner and throttle her—she could feel his fingers tighten round her throat, and see his eyes bulging, his face suffused with blood.

Then it was morning, and she went to the office; and he came in with the insurance invoices and said good morning, just the same as on other mornings; and she said to herself, "Margaret Finlay," she said, "you're a loony, and one of these days you'll end up in the loony bin! You've so got out of the way of meeting people, you don't know what to do any more. This outing will do you the world of good. He's a nice man, Mr Bacon, and just in case he does start being funny you can take a good sharp pen-knife with you, and the girl-guide whistle so that you can get help in a hurry if need be." Then she thought that it would be nice not to go to a café for tea, but to take a picnic—only if the weather was good, of course: and she planned to make egg sandwiches, and tomato sandwiches, and some ginger snaps, perhaps, and the thermos full of tea. Then she got excited, but at the same time felt sick!—just as she used to feel before a party. Then it was Saturday, and she was in a great flurry to finish the housework, and pack the picnic tea before she met him under the great clock at Victoria Station at two.

V

She arrived at three minutes to two, but he was there already in a navy blue raincoat, a newspaper tucked under his arm. He was watching the crowd milling past, but he didn't see her coming. Her heart began to beat very fast and her breath went—as if she'd just cycled up Box Hill without pausing.

"Hallo! Hallo, Mr Bacon!"

"Oh, so there you are. I wasn't quite expecting you yet awhile, Miss Finlay—you've got a couple of minutes yet. Point of fact, you're the most punctual woman I've ever known. What did you bring in the haversack, your watercolours?"

"No, I've brought tea."

"You shouldn't have bothered with that, lass; we could have gone out."

"Well, I thought it would be nice to . . . to have a picnic, and I made some ginger snaps."

"What a lovely idea! I've not had a home-made ginger snap for donkey's years."

"Where do we catch the bus?"

"We don't, lass. I managed to borrow a car—Joe Wilkinson's, to be exact. He's an old shipmate from my navy days. Point of fact, we were on the same ship four years."

"What sort of ship was that?"

"Corvette. We mine-swept the Channel."

"Was that horrible?"

"Sometimes, but there were good times, too. I wasn't lonely then as I am now."

"Don't you keep in touch with your old friends—Mr Wilkinson, for instance?"

"Well, I do, but it's different now. Joe's married and got a couple of kids, you know, and somehow, though they all make me welcome enough and all that, a single man is a bit out of it, you know, a bit out of it . . . Here's the jallopy, lass."

"Oh, it's an Austin!"

"Yes, I might have guessed you'd know all about cars, Miss Finlay."

He held the door open for her. She saw herself, the car having come to a dead stop by the road side, repairing the engine with a deft turn or two of a spanner—"It was just the magneto; very simple to fix"—then she was brought back to earth because she couldn't get her large feet in their sensible brogues into the car. The blood rushed to her face. She wished her feet had been lopped off at birth.

"You're a bit cramped there, aren't you?" said Mr Bacon. "That's the trouble with these old cars, there's no room. Here, lass, try lifting up your legs . . ."

He put his hand under her heels and hoiked them up till her

knees pressed into her tummy. She was in the car, all of her, Margaret Don't-be-so-clumsy Finlay! Desperately, she tried to think of a joke to pass off the incident as he walked round to his side.

"I have huge feet, Mr Bacon; I should have been a policeman!"

He said nothing, pretending to be intent on starting the car. The engine coughed into life with a familiar sound: of course, Daddy had had an Austin, a navy blue one just like this. It was the one he'd driven her to school in, and she'd wanted to sit by him, but Mummy sat there instead. Sometimes he'd let her sit by him when he drove to the village at week-ends. She'd climbed in then with ease.

"My father used to have an Austin just like this, Mr Bacon. That's how I knew it was an Austin—I don't really know much about cars, you know. I didn't have trouble getting my feet in then; I suppose they've grown."

He stared ahead in silence, not knowing what to say. It was her fault, she was embarrassing him. She *always* embarrassed people, even when she tried and tried *not* to embarrass them. "Margaret, you're so gauche, dear! Until you learn how to talk in front of visitors, I think it would be better if you kept your mouth shut. Before you say anything, bite your tongue, and if you still want to say it, bite it again, harder." Mummy had been right: Mummy had the knack of turning out right when she said the most horrid things.

She clenched her fists in her lap and looked through the yellow-stained windshield. They were going down King's Road, a long grey street crowded with people doing their week-end shopping. It was like being imprisoned in a box, sitting in the car. She was looking away from him, but she could hear him breathing close, very close to her.

His hand touched her knee, and she recoiled, thinking of the pen-knife in her handbag and the police whistle, and she wondered how to get them out without his noticing. The walls of the box closed in till she couldn't breathe: she wanted to scream! *Sex maniac throttles City secretary! Woman found mutilated in car!*

"It's a bit cramped, the car, isn't it, Miss Finlay? But the engine's very good considering it's age. Joe and his family have a lot of fun with her. Point of fact, he's looking for a newer one, and I've half a mind to buy the old bus from him. I wouldn't want both a car and a bike, I don't s'pose. A bike would be a sight cheaper to run, but a car would be splendid for jaunts into the country. I love country walks, don't you, Miss Finlay?"

Her body, stripped of its clothing, would be found torn and bleeding in a ditch. There would be a police message on the nine o'clock news: "The police say they are searching for a medium-sized man with thinning red hair who was the last person to be seen in the vicinity. He was wearing a navy-blue raincoat, which he has probably since disposed of."

"I say do you like walking, Miss Finlay?"

"Yes! I mean No! No, I don't!"

"Here, lass, what's up? You aren't sickly, are you?"

"Would you . . . would you please stop the car. I don't feel well!"

He pulled into the side of the road. There were people all round—she was safe!

"Here, Miss Finlay, let me wind down the window. You look as if you need fresh air. Shall I run to a chemist and get you summat?"

"No, no, it's all right. I'll be better in a minute."

"Shall I get you a glass of water?"

"No, really not . . . thank you. I'm so sorry, it was suddenly very stuffy—that's all. I'm better already."

She breathed deeply, taking comfort from the shoppers passing so close—from the fat old lady in a stained black coat, so familiar, dangling the shopping nets, bulging with groceries, from her wrists. "Margaret Finlay," she said to herself, "you're a great goose! I'm ashamed of you—thoroughly ashamed!"

"Shall I drive you back home, Miss Finlay?"

"No, please don't. I am sorry I was such a silly, but I suddenly felt sick. I think it was being in a car again after such a long time, and being in a car so like Daddy's. It upset me, I suppose. But I'm all right now, Mr Bacon, do drive on again!"

"Right you are, lass, if you say so. If it's not a personal question, Miss Finlay, has your father passed away?"

"Oh, no, he's in India. I've just not seen him since I was a little girl, that's all."

"Why's that? if you'll excuse me asking..."

"Well... he married again, you see, and he and his wife live in Bombay, and they just haven't been back to England. They may come one day, I suppose; one day."

"What about your mother?"

"Oh, she's married again, too. They live in the south of France somewhere."

"You must be a bit lonely with no family."

"Sometimes. I don't give a button for *her*, of course, but I do wish Daddy would write to me. There was only him and Gran, and he's married and doesn't write, and Gran's dead. Perhaps, one day I'll go out to India to see him—when I've saved up enough!"

"Look, Miss Finlay," he said, hesitantly. "We're both very lonely people, aren't we? And I want to tell you that I like you very much, because I feel that you're one of the few people in this city that I can trust. I want you to feel you can trust me, Miss Finlay, because I'd like you for my friend."

"Why—thank you, Mr Bacon. Thanks ever so much! I mean I do trust you, really I do. I was only being silly when I got faint. I mean I've not told anyone about my parents, not anyone. I don't really know why it came out like that . . ."

"But I feel I can talk to you, too, Miss Finlay. You're different, somehow, and I feel you'll be able to understand when others won't. I'd like you to tell me all about your family and friends, and so on, if you'd like to; and I'd like to tell you about myself—if it wouldn't be boring to you to hear me—and I'd like you to feel that you have a good friend in me. I feel I'd like to be a good friend to you, Miss Finlay . . ."

"I'd like you to be my friend, too, Mr Bacon, and . . . I'd like to be your friend. I'm sorry . . . that I'm so wretchedly shy; I always have been, and I've always found it very difficult to make friends with people. But I do like you, Mr Bacon, and I will try, I promise I will."

"Thanks very much, thanks very much indeed; I appreciate it and want you to know that I do. Look, let's begin by calling each other by first names. My name's Herbert, and I wish you'd call me it."

"My name's Margaret. Do call me Margaret, Mr Ba . . ."

"Now, not Mr Bacon, Margaret; *Herbert*."

"Right-o . . . Herbert! Oh, Putney Bridge! Where are we going? I thought we were going to St Albans."

"I've taken the liberty of altering our plans without previously consulting you. I want to drive you to Chanctonbury Ring. It's a bit further, but not very much. We'll be there by tea-time—if that's all right. We can be back in town by seven or thereabouts, in case you have an appointment."

"That's quite all right, I don't have to be back for anyone. Chanctonbury Ring's in Sussex, isn't it? I went to school near there. I love the downs, but I never went to Chanctonbury. I went to Steyning and Arundel, but never Chanctonbury. I don't know why. I'd love to go, Mr Bac—Herbert."

"Right you are, lass, anchors away—we're embarked."

VI

He parked the car on the grass verge at the side of the slate-coloured lane, and she manœuvred herself out. It was a fine spring afternoon, and she could smell the salt of the sea—a fine, clean smell brought by a brisk breeze across the downs. It was a smell that she was used to, and it carried with it many associations, both pleasant and unpleasant—long Sunday walks by herself when she got to be a senior at St Faith's; hockey on spring afternoons; rambles and picnics on the downs. She closed her eyes for a moment, and felt just like a schoolgirl again. "Now, girls, you may wander off on your own, but don't wander too far; and when you hear me blow three blasts on my whistle, come straight back!" Miss Blandford, the guidemistress. Margaret had been a *Petrel*—she had forgotten that . . .

"Give you a penny for them lass."

"I was just thinking how I used to be a guide, that's all. I was a *Petrel*, I remember. We used to go for hikes over the downs—that's what reminded me."

"I was an Eagle in the Scouts:

> Oh, once I was an Eagle—
> A jolly fine Eagle, too;
> But now I've given up eagling
> I don't know what to do—"

His voice was flat as a corn-crake, but she remembered the song, and with the last few lines she joined in:

> "I'm growing old and feeble,
> And I can sing no more,
> So I'm going back to Gilwell, if I can . . ."

"Well, lass, I didn't know you would know it. Neither of us are grand-opera, point of fact . . ."

"But we don't do too badly," she finished for him. "Oh, look," she said, pointing. There were three egg-shaped hills, the first of which was crowned with a circle of dark trees. It was like the tonsured head of a Tibetan monk . . .

"What did you say, lass?"

"Oh, I didn't realise I was talking out loud. I was just thinking that that hill with the tuft of woods at the top was like the head of a Tibetan monk!—bare, you know, except for the tuft of hair on the top."

"I wouldn't know, lass, I've never seen one."

"Nor have I, actually, only I've *imagined* them."

"You're a great one for dreaming, I should say," said Herbert Bacon, and he looked at her with eyes surprisingly hot and blue— they reminded her extraordinarily of Daddy's eyes! What did he mean, she was a great one for dreaming?

"Come along, Margaret, we've got to get to the top and down before night-fall, and at this rate we're going to take all of next week!"

VII

At first they walked abreast of one another, chatting easily of this and that, but soon the ascent took most of their breath. The path took a meandering circle, and Herbert Bacon, a man of direct action, left it with a quizzical nod to climb the hill-side direct. The South Downs breeze blew Margaret's hair across her flushed cheeks—she was enjoying the exercise as she hadn't enjoyed riding her bicycle in months.

Herbert's step was steady enough, but he was breathing like

an old donkey-engine—much more heavily than she was. She was going to make some comment about his being out of condition, and how cycling would improve his wind, but she thought that such a remark would be in questionable taste. Under the circumstances, bragging was out of place, and she might very well hurt his feelings by it. So she saved her breath, and was in a very short time glad she'd thought better of such cheap wit, needing all the wind she could get for herself.

She was climbing to the top of Chanctonbury, as she had climbed the rockery that was also the Himalayas—to banish the blight from the accursed lands. What an odd thought, what on earth did she mean by it? When one was taking hard physical exercise all sorts of nonsense raced through the mind. Panting up a hill in Sussex behind Herbert Bacon was hard work, and it had no bearing on the miserable rockery at Aylestone House, or, on the other hand, on some snow-capped peaks in Tibet. All she was in quest of was—well, friendship, really. She had decided that she was too much by herself, and that she should make more effort to mix with people. He had asked her out to lunch, and then to go and take some brass-rubbings at St Albans; they had changed their minds, and had come to Sussex instead. He was a nice man, simple and sincere, and he behaved like a perfect gentleman with her—very different from his somewhat vulgar chaffing in the typists' room. She liked his Yorkshire accent—there was something homely and honest about it.

Why had he brought her here? Because he was lonely, and had found no one to talk to in London. This was understandable—London was a very lonely city. She herself had lived for years in London, and knew hardly a soul.

It was very nice spending a Saturday afternoon with someone else for a change. Perhaps, when Herbert got his bicycle, they could go for expeditions lasting all day long. They could leave very early, for now that the weather was improving, it would be a pleasure to set out at six in the morning. They could cycle up to sixty miles from London easily, and still return before night. What a silly-billy she had been in the car, with her foolish terrors of his nefarious intentions, and her readiness to reach for her pen-knife and guide-whistle; and all the while he was an old scout himself.

This hill was like life. As she had thought it would be difficult to meet people and get to know them, so the hill had seemed steep; but when you tackled the problem of friendship with the same directness with which Herbert Bacon climbed the hill, the difficulties disappeared beneath your feet, and you emerged triumphant (if breathless) on the very summit.

They were nearly at the ring of trees themselves—a fuzz of charcoal against the April sky, but flecked with tiny lime-green buds. He turned to her smiling; he was rather pale, and she could see that for him climbing the hill had been rather an effort. He nodded to her to look at the view, and she turned from him—it was only polite to give him a chance to get his breath.

Before her was a great saucer of patchwork fields, rimmed by a distant line of blue hills that must be, she supposed, the Surrey Downs. Immediately below, at the foot of the great mounds they now stood on, the grey lane, flanked with lettuce-coloured hedges, wound its way to a village of mellow roofs set amidst pocket handkerchief plots; from which rose a square Norman tower and spire, etched in light and shadow, protected from the sea winds by the smooth-curving, rough-tufted chalk downs on which they stood. The view was certainly not as heroic as from cloud-capped peaks in distant Tibet, but there was a feeling of orderliness and gentle fertility about this valley, a quality ineffably English, that gave it a beauty far more real, and far more appealing than the dramatic crests of the imagination.

And did those feet in ancient time
Walk upon England's mountains green?
And was the holy lamb of God
On England's pleasant pastures seen?

"Well, lass, shall we sit down?" Mr Bacon asked. He had evidently recovered his breath and felt the view had been admired long enough.

"Of course," she said, and promptly squatted on the coarse grass.

"Hey there, lass, you don't want to catch a chill. You'd best sit on my raincoat."

"It's quite all right, thanks, I never catch chills—I'm as strong as a horse!"

"Do as I say, lass, and don't be obstinate."

"But your mack'll get muddied."

"It's muddy already; besides, this stuff brushes off easily enough."

"But where will you sit?"

"I'll sit alongside—there's plenty of room."

He grunted, and sat down too close to her, so that his knees touched hers. She drew her knees aside and pulled down her tweed skirt over them. She was conscious of his breathing, and of a smell of sweat and tobacco—a nasty smell—that was about him. She didn't want to look at him, so she stared down into the valley. There was a chimney smoking from a grey house set amidst trees. Why did people need a fire on such a warm afternoon, she wondered. It was unpatriotic somehow, for even though there was no war there was still a fuel shortage, and every knob of coal that such people so heedlessly burnt had to be hewed out of the living rock by someone. How selfish people were! How wasteful and thoughtless!

"I don't want to hint, lass," Mr Bacon said, "but in Yorkshire we're very blunt, you know, and after that climb I feel kind of peckish. As a matter of fact I didn't have much lunch. I'm so empty you could hear a dried pea rattle in my innards!"

"Yes, of course," she said, trying to hide the slight distaste she felt at his crudity by busying herself with her haversack. "Here's a packet of sandwiches; please help yourself."

"Thanks very much, lass—by goom, this was a splendid idea of yours!" He rustled the wax paper voluptuously—she could tell by the thickness of his voice that his mouth was watering. It disgusted her! She shrank from him to the extreme edge of his raincoat.

"Where're you going, lass? Now don't go and sit on the grass, I told you. Here, have one."

"No, thank you very much, I'm really not terribly hungry."

"Now, don't be silly, woman, take one."

"No, thank you, I couldn't eat it."

"Look, if you don't eat one, neither will I. You'll make me think you've poisoned them, that's what! Now, coom on, Margaret lass; take one and eat it up. Little girls who don't eat their sandwiches, don't grow into fine tall women! Here you are—eat it and let's have no more of your nonsense."

He handed her a sandwich, and obediently she took a bite out of it. It was as dry as chalk. He was masticating his noisily, like a dog eating out of a bowl. She felt slightly sick.

"By gum, these are capital, lass. What are they, curd-cheese and onion?"

"Cream cheese and chives."

"Are they now. Isn't that a coincidence? My mother always made us cream-cheese—curd-cheese we call it—by letting the milk go solid-sour, and then letting it drip through a cloth. It was great stuff. You know, this takes me right back to the old days—it's funny how the taste of summat, or a smell, can do that, isn't it? Do you find that, too?"

"I don't know, really." He was champing again. She wished she hadn't brought sandwiches. She was conscious of his knees: she was conscious of his somewhat crumpled, somewhat moist flannel trousers. He had perspired a lot climbing the hill—and he smelt of old pea-soup!

"... we used to get home from school at four-thirty. Then, I'd get on my bicycle and do my paper round in Oaks—I delivered the morning and evening papers in a rather swell district, you see ... to help out Mother. She worked as a cleaning woman to keep me in school. It was hard, though you never heard a word of complaint from her. Well, after the rounds, I'd come straight home for me tea, and she would allus have a bite of something hot—a grilled kipper, like, or a fried egg or summat; and then there'd be home-baked bread and jam, or curd-cheese like this lot here, or golden syrup. I'd stuff and stuff—I'd never had much lunch nobbut a crust of bread, and a swallow of water, and I was hungry. After tea, I'd join the other lads in the street for a game of soccer, or cricket, or cowboys-and-injuns, or hide-and-seek; or just a good old gang-fight, hell-for-leather! Lordy," he guffawed, blowing onion-gas and wet crumbs over her, "we were a rough lot! The number of windows we smashed would make a sizeable hot-house!" He continued to guffaw at the memory, and he put a hand on her knee. She felt she was going to faint! She had to escape! She *had* to escape!

"Did you play games as a bairn, Margaret? Grandmother's footsteps, or hide-and-seek-stuff like that?"

"Yes, oh yes," she said desperately. "Hide-and-seek was my favourite. Do let's play now!" She sprang up and moved away out of his reach.

"But we've not finished tea, lass," he protested in apparent astonishment. "Besides, we'll look proper fools playing hide-and-seek at our age..."

"That doesn't matter, it doesn't matter at all. You finish your tea, and I'll run off and hide. Count up to two hundred—no, five hundred, and then you can look for me."

"You're just kidding—aren't you? Up North, we say, 'I'm going off to powder me nose'—if you're a woman, that is; and if you're a man you say, 'I've to pay a visit to aunty.' Here, hold on a minute," he was shouting now. "You don't really want me to play *Hi*—do you?"

"... Count up to five hundred then come and look!" she called from the fringe of the woods.

"Right you are," he shouted, "and if I shout, 'All hands on deck!' it's because someone is coming; then we meet back here, by my raincoat."

"All right," she called, and ran into the heart of the forest.

VIII

Forest? No, it was the thinnest of copses, with prickly tangle-brush under foot, and stunted little trees, too meagre to afford much protection. She did the best she could, crouching on her knees amidst the dried up leaves and twigs, behind a reasonably substantial beech. The leaves smelt of death; she wished a hole would show itself—a sort of fairy rabbit-warren—so that she could shrink up small and crawl into it. She would have a lid made to pull down over herself which would look to the rest of the world like a bramble. She would be able to hear them walking around, but they'd never, never be able to find her...

"Coo-ee," she heard Mr Bacon call, "Coo-ee!" There was a crunching of leaves, one-two, one-two—how sounds carried!

She searched round for a better place of concealment but there was none. The terrible crunching and shuffling was nearer now! A thrush on the branch in front of her, beady-eyed and sharp-beaked, watched. He jerked his head as if in affirmation, and flew off in a flurry of wings.

"Coo-ee!" Herbert Bacon called—he was closer, much closer! "I'm getting warm, Margaret lass . . ."

Her heart fluttered in her throat as if she had swallowed the thrush alive and it was stuck there. Mr Bacon was a man of direct action! A man of method! He would find her—it was certain he would find her! Quick, the pen-knife—oh, horrors! she'd left them in her bag by the raincoat. Oh, silly, silly girl! Hide! Hide! For heaven's sake, hide!

Six inches from her nose, half buried under one of the oak's roots, was a crumpled and dirty carton that had contained *Player's* cigarettes. The ruddy and bearded sailor was defiled by streaks of mud. People were filthy! Revolting! Why could they never hide their refuse? She stuffed the sailor with his richly chestnut beard under the root.

"Coo-ee, I'm going to get you, Margaret Finlay. You can't hide from me!"

He was all but on top of her. Frantically, she clawed leaves and top soil spreading them over the hole where she had hidden the sailor—she must have him buried before they discovered her! She *must*!

Miss Pritchard was coming to find her! Miss Pritchard was going to murder Bradshaw! Miss Pritchard would send her to Mummy, and Mummy to the Head and they would all attack her: "Margaret, you're absolutely *filthy*!" "Margaret, you're a nasty little horror! No wonder you have no friends, Margaret!" "Margaret, people who talk to themselves end up in the mad-house—you're going *mad*, Margaret Finlay, mad!"

"Coo-ee!" "Coo-ee!"

She tensed herself like an animal at bay, waiting with quivering flanks for the whole pack of dogs, the witch-woman with her cruel bullets, Miss Pritchard with her lips tight with anger, the Head with her searchlight eyes, Matron, Mrs Fleisch, Gladys Peach, Norma Gracewell—all conspiring together to plan her end; all licking their sharp teeth ready to tear into her throat...

"No!" she croaked—"Dear God, no!"

"Caught you, Margaret Finlay! I told you I would—didn't I?"

There was no shot. There were no dogs leaping for her windpipe. Only, there was Herbert Bacon, and he was smiling at her, and offering her his hand to help her to her feet.

"What's up, lass?" he asked—"you look a bit sickly again! Are you all right?"

"Oh yes," she said, and her heart bounded with joy and relief—she was alive and unhurt, and Herbert Bacon was not her enemy. He was her dear friend, her boon-companion, and she had not recognised him. She was a great goose.

"Do you know what, Herbert? I am a great goose! A great goose!"

"Why d'you say that?"

"Because I am! I'll race you back to the raincoat, last one home is a silly sausage!"

She picked up her tweed skirt and ran like the wind, leaping over hummocks and tree logs like a thoroughbred jumper. She won by ten seconds at least—the first race she had ever won in her life, and she had known she would win. Poor Herbert was quite winded! She had to smile, though plainly he was rather peeved.

"Look," she said, "you found me so quickly, I just *had* to win the race." She was overcome with breathless giggling, and Herbert, mollified in spite of himself, had to giggle with her.

"Look, Margaret lass," he said, "we're about to be overrun with girl-guides—I can see a troop of them coming up the path. You're one of them, but I'm not, and they make me feel uncomfortable, so let's be off!"

He gathered up his coat and her haversack.

"Just one more look at the view," she begged.

They stood in silence, the great and fertile valley falling from their feet. The sun was sinking, the colours deepening, and the Surrey hills were only a purple haze. It was as if they had been together a long time ago on an island of golden sand that glittered in the sunlight; they had started a long voyage together, only to be separated by a dreadful storm; after the storm there had been nothing but thick grey fog, and her voice in loneliness crying for him had echoed back on itself in mockery: until now, when after much sorrow and travail, they stood side by side on the topmost mountain, surveying the richness of their kingdom.

Soon, soon, they would embark on the long white ship, which would bear them swiftly to wheresoever they wished, on a voyage, perhaps, which would circumnavigate the entire demesne. They would visit the palaces and cathedrals, the gardens and parks, the deepest forests and the highest mountains; and they would bring to all their subjects, rich and poor, the joyous message that the land was at last freed from the witch-queen's curse, and all the bells would be rung day and night for a week.

For they had found the precious flower; they had triumphed at last against the whole host of their innumerable enemies. Now, as long as they believed in each other, their enemies were powerless. The moment of victory, after so many dangers and tribulations, was sweet.

Margaret closed her eyes the better to savour it, and the blaze of light from the sinking sun turned the lids from darkness to rich amber.

"Oh, life is going to be so *good*!" she murmured out loud.

"I was just thinking the same thing, Margaret, lass."

She opened her eyes to be dazzled by the sun's orange blaze, and she turned to him:

"Now I've found you," she whispered, "you won't disappear, will you?"

"No, Margaret Finlay, I'll not disappear—unless you tell me to."

"Thank you," she said, and added—"Dear-heart," but so quietly he couldn't hear.

"Thank you," he said. "Now I don't know about you, Margaret Finlay, but I for one am getting chilly. Would you fancy a cup of tea?"

"Lovely!" she said, "and boiled eggs, and brown bread and watercress, and scones and strawberry jam—I'm starving, Herbert!"

"And here coom the bluebottles," he said, and nodded at the shrilling, skipping, swarming flock of guides, in their midst a broad-shouldered, deep-chested shepherd, in a blue tunic, green tie, and black, broad-brimmed hat. She raised a whistle to her lips, and sent a piercing blast over Sussex.

"Come on," whispered Herbert to Margaret, and grabbing her arm, he ran her laughing and protesting, down the steep hill-side, till they both all but fell, Jack and Jill-like, on their crowns. Then, the pair of them, exhausted, but possessed of the very secret of happiness, walked slowly down the cart-track to the car.

IX

It was Margaret who found the tea-rooms—a grey-stone cottage with a notice in the latticed windows: Lunches, teas, and light refreshments. There was a long, low, dark-beamed room, with polished oak tables laid for tea, and on the wall cottagey pictures, pieces of brass, and old clocks. The proprietress was a Yorkshire woman, a brisk old lady with a ruddy face, her iron-grey hair pulled behind her ears into a bun. She and Herbert exchanged Yorkshireisms for a while, then she bustled out into the kitchen to return presently with a loaded tray. Margaret and Herbert, both hungry after their exertions, exchanged little conversation till they had satisfied the inner man; but their silence was a comfortable silence. Margaret marvelled that she felt so much at ease with this funny little man, having known him for so short a while.

When they had emptied all the plates and were down to draining the brown, earthenware teapot, Herbert asked her if he might light his pipe. That was why she liked him, she decided: he made her feel a lady, fragile, delicate, and pampered, instead of an overgrown schoolgirl.

The blue smoke of bis briar spiralled to the raftered ceiling, and like a genie from the *Arabian Nights*, he made all sorts of strange faces and wonderful scenes appear from it. She saw him clearly enough across the clutter of tea things, in time present. He was lounging back in his chair, legs crossed comfortably, his nicotined, stubby, strong fingers caressing the bowl of his pipe. His gingerish eyebrows were shaggy, his white collar was frayed, his R.N.V.R. tie—wavy red and white lines against a dark blue background—was shiny but sprucely knotted. All this she saw with an intense clarity. But she saw also a brisk old lady with the upright carriage of a soldier—not unlike the proprietress of the tea-room—scurrying about a tiny house that stood at the end of a long row of houses just like it, face to face with one row, and back to back with another. Street after street of tiny grey houses with smoking chimneys which breathed soot into the grey pall which overhung the city, so that the air itself was foul, griming every leaf, greying every face, eating into the living lungs of a proud, clean-living people, bright spirits under a cloud of machine-age filth. And the brightest of spirits, Herbert's mother, Mrs Bacon, keeping her house clean and comfortable, the curtains freshly washed, the windows sparkling, however heavy the cloud without.

The day's work was done; all morning Mrs Bacon had scrubbed and polished for Councillor Grimsby's wife, and all afternoon for Mrs Blackburn whose husband owned one of the great mills. At five o'clock she had come, her arms laden with shopping, to do her own housework, and to make dinner for her son. They had eaten the fragrant stew, wiping up the gravy with crusty bread. They had done the dishes. The two of them sat on either side of the small, glowing grate, she darning socks and dreaming of her son's future, he bent in concentration over his homework. The fire crackled, the kettle sang on the hob, the oaken clock—Mrs Bacon's only inheritance from her father, once a well-to-do farmer—ticked comfortably through the evening.

There was a rough knocking at the door. Mrs Bacon looked up in alarm, the darning motionless in her lap. "Don't open it, Ma," pleaded the little boy who was Herbert—"Ma, I tell you don't open it." She paid no attention, and unlatching the only barrier between them and a big, drunken bully, dark-jowelled, bleary-eyed, foul of breath and language, who only departed when he had the savings from the old treacle tin on the mantelpiece in his pocket. Why didn't she hide the money from him? Why, indeed, did she open the door to him at all? Because she lived by a rigid principle that joined a man and his wife for better for worse, for richer for poorer, till death did them part, and because the principle of steadfast loyalty was more important than the blustering of a drunken lout who took all and gave nothing.

The scene changed: the proud spirit was at peace in her coffin, her eyes closed, her hands crossed, her duty done. As the coffin was being lowered into its pit in the bleak, sooty, unlovely graveyard, a red-headed boy was blinded by hot tears, and choked by the bitter grief that swelled in his throat. A handful of neighbours, stoic and grim-faced women mostly, who had learned to expect nothing but suffering, and who accepted this logical end to a hard life as they would accept their own, stood round the grave, their black-shawled heads bowed in respect. The drink-sodden brute who was this woman's husband, who gave her his child, who lived for so many years on her meagre earnings, was not there. Councillor Grimsby's wife had sent a small laurel wreath; Mrs Blackburn had sent a bunch of tawny chrysanthemums.

Then there was Violet, a sort of snake-woman, that held Herbert under some terrible spell—she must have been like Mummy, only common, of course, as Norma Gracewell was common. Too much lipstick; cheap perfume; cheap satin blouses over cheap satin slip, and fat calves gleaming in cheap silk stockings. The honeymoon at Blackpool?—but the picture became vague, and Margaret was conscious of his staring at his dead pipe without seeing it. They had had only one night of a honeymoon; then he had to rejoin his ship, for it was one of those wartime marriages. He was a sub-lieutenant then, and very proud of his commission—a self-educated man amongst born gentlemen—and he went for nine months duty mine-sweeping in the North Sea with a high heart. Then he returned on an unexpected ten days leave—the ship in dock for repairs—to find an American airforce cap and greatcoat in the hall, and in his bedroom . . . ?

She had an absurd picture of Mummy sitting up in bed with Captain Hillyard—but she soon put an end to that by having Matron come in and clap her hands. Then Margaret Finlay was back with Herbert Bacon again.

"I'm so sorry your marriage was a failure," she said.

"You needn't be," he said, "I had it coming to me. Point of fact, I was lucky there wasn't a child to make matters worse . . ."

She had a ludicrous picture of Margaret lying on her bed at school, stark naked, by the prostrate corpse of a pony. And Matron watching, having not the least idea of what was happening, seeing only a new girl undressed—Margaret had to smile; she just had to smile.

Herbert Bacon was looking at her oddly—of course! How could he possibly understand what she was smiling at, and how could she possibly explain, *if he didn't understand without her telling him*? It would be as bad as telling someone that you thought they were dead!

"I . . . I was just thinking how splendid it is to have . . . to have someone to talk to," she said. "No one has ever talked to me like this before, you know, except for . . ."

"For whom Margaret?"

"Well, except for no one, really. It 's all been such fun, today."

"Hasn't it, lass—hide-and-seek and all. I've not had such a day for years! And you might as well know that I've never told a soul else what I've just told you. I'm not in the habit of opening up my heart to every Tom, Dick or Harry, you know."

"I'm . . . I'm honoured by your confidence," she said.

"I'm honoured to give it you. I hope you'll give me yours."

"I'll try. I really will try."

"The only thing that scares me," he said, "is the thought of waking up in London on Monday morning, and getting to Boothby's, and finding you Miss Finlay again, and that all this was just a dream. It's all been like a sort of fairy-story, lass—for me at any rate."

"For me, too," she said gravely.

"But we can do summat similar next Saturday afternoon—can't we, lass?"

"Indeed, we can," she answered.

Chapter Five

I

On Monday morning, Margaret Finlay arrived at Boothby's at ten minutes to ten instead of nine-thirty. But she had steeled herself against her reception.

"Good morning, Mrs Fleisch, good morning Gladys, good morning Norma!"

There was a moment of silent stupefaction in the typists' room as Margaret took off her old khaki raincoat. In spite of her good resolutions she blushed.

Mrs Fleisch was the first to recover:

"But it's a new dress," she cried. "Now I understand why you are coming late. We were all worried, Miss Finlay: we thought you had had an accident . . . "

"It's the first time since I bin here you've come in after me," said Norma.

"I stopped at Selfridges on the way—they're having a spring sale," Margaret explained.

"Turn around, Miss Finlay, and let's have a proper look," said Gladys. "Oh, the skirt's *bouffong*! Isn't it a little dressy for biking?'"

"But I like it, Miss Finlay," cried Mrs Fleisch. "It is a charming material—is it silk?"

"No," said Margaret, "as a matter of fact it's nylon. You don't have to iron it, they say."

"Oh, but you do," said Gladys; "it looks sort of rumpled if you don't."

"It looks ever so funny seeing you in a dress," said Norma. "I don't think I've ever seen you in a dress before, Miss Finlay."

"Norma," said Mrs Fleisch, "you are now personal to the point of impertinence..."

"Ow, but I don't mean it like that—you know that, Miss Finlay, don't you? I think it's a smashin' dress, honest I do. It makes you look ever so much younger."

"May I ask what are you paying for this, Miss Finlay?" asked Mrs Fleisch.

"Well," Margaret replied, "guess." She giggled, hating her coyness.

"But I have no idea," said Mrs Fleisch. "Five pounds? Ten pounds?"

"Thirty-nine and eleven," cried Margaret triumphantly.

"No," cried Mrs Fleisch, "but that is fantastic. Have they any left? Any in my size, I mean?"

"Oh, they had lots twenty minutes ago," said Margaret, "in all sorts of sizes and colours. The only thing is there were rather a lot of people looking at them..."

"Mrs Fleisch," said Gladys, "do you think we could take our lunch-hour now?"

"But we cannot, Gladys," said Mrs Fleisch. "Who will take Mr Gold's dictation?"

"I'll hold the fort for you, Mrs Fleisch," said Margaret.

"Glad, be a sport..."

"Norm, be an angel..." Norma and Gladys said in unison.

"Toss you for it," said Norm; "heads I win, tails you lose..."

"None of your teddy-girl tricks with me, thank you very much, Miss Gracewell. If we toss a coin, I'll be the one to do it. O.K.?"

"No, you cheat," said Norma. "I only pretend to cheat. Miss

Finlay would you toss for us?"

"I—I can try," Margaret said, "if both of you trust me, that is."

"O.K. by me," said Norma.

"All right," said Gladys.

"Heads, Norma, tails Gladys—right?"

"Right," the girls agreed.

Margaret took a penny from the pocket of her raincoat, and flicked it in the air—as Monica Humphries used to do as the skipper of netball at St Faith's.

"It's tails," she said. "That's you, Gladys, isn't it?"

"She gets all the luck," Norma grumbled. "Still, I haven't got any money anyway."

After Mrs Fleisch and Gladys had whirled out of the office, Norma sat quietly in her chair, nibbling her thumbnail and staring. Margaret was aware of it, very aware, but she carried on as usual on a Monday, sorting out Friday's contracts for filing.

"Miss Finlay, may I ask you a question?"

"I think so, Norma," Margaret replied a little nervously.

"Is your Mr Bradshaw the real thing?"

Norma's dark little eyes were as bright with curiosity as a sparrow's. Margaret forced herself to look away. She began checking through her contracts once more.

"I don't quite know what you mean by 'the real thing,' Norma," she answered.

"I mean was it love at first sight?" said Norma.

"Yes, yes, I think I can say it was," Margaret answered.

"How old were you then, Miss Finlay?"

"I was eight," Margaret answered. "I was in bed with the measles."

"And he fell for you just the same, all covered with them spots?"

Margaret couldn't help smiling at Norma's stupefaction.

"Yes, Norma, he did. He seemed never to notice them."

"And he's loved you ever since?"

"Yes, he has."

"What about now? I mean is it the same thing now he's come back after all these years?"

"No, Norma, it isn't. But how could it be? I'm older now—much older."

"But he still feels the same?"

Bradshaw nodded vigorously.

"Yes, my dear, Bradshaw still feels the same."

Norma sighed.

"Honest," she said, "I dunnow how you do it. I've never been able to keep 'em interested more than six months."

"What about your American friend, Norma?"

"That's what I mean, see? Look, Miss Finlay, if I tell you suthink will you keep it to yourself?"

"Why, of course, Norma, if you want." What else could she say?

"Well, everythink's fixed for Johnny and me to get married, but now we've gone and got the wind up, the pair of us. We went out yesterday and it was awful. I didn't know what to say to him or him to me—d'you know what I mean? We just 'adn't got anythink to say to each other, that's all. I mean, what do I do, Miss Finlay? I mean, how do I 'old him?"

"Well, Norma," Margaret replied, "I don't know. I'm the last person in the world to give you advice like that, you know I . . ."

"But you're not, Miss Finlay. I mean I can't ask anyone else—can I?"

"What about Gladys?"

"What, that little cat? I wouldn't give her the satisfaction."

"Well, what about Mrs Fleisch?"

"She might, but you're the one I want," said Norma. "You're so mysterious. While all the rest of us talk boys, boys, boys, showing off like anythink, you just keep yourself to yourself and suddenly come out with a Hollywood film star who's been in love with you for years. Now, come on, be a sport and tell how you did it? Did you flirt with other men?"

"Never," said Margaret emphatically.

"Not even just to tease him a bit?"

"I never teased Bradshaw—except when he knew I was teasing; nor did he ever tease me. We both thought exactly what we said."

Norma giggled—"You mean you said exactly what you thought, don't you? Did you talk much?"

"Oh, yes, we talked for hours."

"What about?"

"Oh, about all the things we'd done; about our families and other people—whether we liked them or not; about all the things we wanted to do together."

"Did you talk all the time?"

"By no means. There were long silences, but we always knew what each other was thinking; we never *had* to speak."

"Ow, how loverly," Norma sighed. "I dunnow what Johnny's thinkin' at all unless he's making love—necking I mean. You know, I tease Glad a bit, but I'm a good girl."

"I'm sure you are, Norma..."

"But now I dunnow what to do, Miss Finlay, honest. I've 'ad all my own way till now with boys, but now I'm scared. It's all because I'm so nuts about him, I suppose. I don't think I ought to let him see it, do you?"

"I just don't know, Norma."

"But did you never pretend just a little with Bradshaw? I mean, just for him not to think you was too easy to catch?"

"I always told the truth to Bradshaw, even when I hid it from other people. I pretended *with* Bradshaw, but never against him."

"Did you tell him just everythink?" asked Norma in apparent amazement.

"Whatever he wanted to know," Margaret replied.

"Did he tell you everything you wanted to know?"

"Yes."

"Did you ask him about other women—I mean seeing he was in Hollywood with all them film stars?"

What an extraordinary question!

"It never occurred to me to ask him, Norma. I didn't want to know more than he told me of his own free will."

"But aren't you jealous of other women?"

"No, I don't think so. Why should I be?"

"Well, how are you sure he's really yours?"

Margaret smiled.

"Well, that I do know," she answered. "He couldn't be anyone else's. It just isn't possible."

"But how do you know?"

"I just do. We've never lied to each other, and there's no reason for us to begin now. If we can't be frank at least with one another, whom can we be frank with?"

"D'you think that's how I should treat Johnny?"

"Norma, I just don't know about other people—I never have. But it does seem to me that any—any friendship between two people that isn't based on truth isn't worth very much."

"I s'pose you're right, Miss Finlay. All right, well I won't play Johnny up then, but I'm not going to go all mushy neither."

"Well—I wish you luck."

"Thanks ever so, Miss Finlay, you've bin ever so nice . . ."

"Oh, rot . . ."

"No, it isn't rot, you have been nice, so there!" cried Norma. "But will you tell me one more thing?"

"If I can, Norma?"

"Did you have a loverly week-end, Miss Finlay?"

Margaret couldn't help smiling.

"Yes, I did," she said, "it was perfect."

"I knew you 'ad," Norma said. "You look quite different somehow..."

"It's just the new dress..."

"No, it isn't. It's more than that," Norma insisted. "Miss Finlay, will you be my friend?"

What a strange child Norma was! A lump came into Margaret's throat for no reason at all, and she couldn't speak. It was extraordinary!

"I just like talking to you, Miss Finlay, that's all. May I?"

Margaret groped for words.

"Of course," she said. "I—I should like to be your friend, Norma."

II

For the pair of them, then, spring grew into an enchanted summer, and it seemed to Margaret that never before had she been so aware of the beauty of a fine May in London.

She was woken in the mornings by the sunlight that poured into her room. On the way to work, the sun glittered on her chrome handlebars, dazzling her. It mellowed sooty red brick and grey stone, and made the pavements sparkle. The sun shone full in the pale faces of Londoners, so that they had to screw up their eyes, and then, in spite of themselves, smile at their own grimaces, before they scurried into the familiar artificial lighting of underground or office building.

City men discarded their shroud-like overcoats and black hats to saunter bare-headed in pearl-grey, as if Fenchurch Street was *Les Bois de Boulogne*. City women burst into flowered dresses, white shoes and gloves, and their white hats were adorned with bunches of violets and clusters of roses.

All the trees had bright leaves of tender green: the stunted little elms of Victoria so dear to dogs, the tall chestnuts of the parks, the great oaks deep-rooted in the grass moat surrounding the Tower. Everything was shining; everywhere was green, white, red, yellow, and purple.

Everyone in the office went mad on flowers. Mrs Fleisch, whose wedding had been postponed till October, appeared in a parchment linen suit ornamented with enormous pearl buttons, and she bore a great armful of purple lilac. Gladys, whose wedding had been postponed till September, appeared in pink stripes rather too snug for her dumpy hips, and tastefully arranged a chipped teacupful of violets on her desk. Norma, who was now getting married in December, danced into the typists' room slender as a jonquil, in a white sleeveless blouse, very low-cut, and a swirling, mustard-yellow skirt, with two dozen yellow tea-roses cocooned in Bond Street florist's tissue—a tribute from her American Air Force lover that made Gladys Peach speechless with fury for an entire morning. Margaret herself, suddenly relaxing her twelve years' reserve, carried in one Monday morning a sheaf of white syringa branches that she and Herbert had clipped the afternoon before, off a tree bordering a twisting Hertfordshire lane. She arranged them in one of the cleaner's buckets on the filing cabinet; and the scent of lilacs, roses, and syringa mingled till they were almost intoxicating. "Just like a bloomin' funeral," Norma said, with an aptness that made Margaret smile.

Margaret started behaving like a magazine heroine, and when she muttered to herself that she was being an extravagant lunatic, all she did was giggle—it was as if a leprechaun had taken possession of all her common sense. She filled the room in Ebury Street with flowers—syringa, sweet-breathed jonquils, and a water-jug full of great daffodils yellow as butter. One Saturday morning she cycled to Oxford Street, where she bought in rapid succession no less than three summer dresses—one white, one blue, and one yellow—a shady white hat, and even white lace gloves. She paid for the lot with a cheque, giving instructions that it was all to be sent as quickly as possible to Ebury Street. Her *Grande Dame* self-assurance astonished herself, and she thought that even Mummy would be astonished could she have seen her only daughter. The idea made her giggle again in sheer exhilaration, and before she knew where she was she had bought in addition a white blouse almost as daring as Norma's, a blue and white striped skirt, a white handbag, and a huge bottle of Yardley's lavender water, all of which she took with her in her saddle-bag to wear that very afternoon when she went to Kew Gardens with Herbert.

She and Herbert went out every Saturday afternoon and all day Sunday. Every week-day they met for a picnic lunch at one sharp. They often went to the Tower embankment to watch the slow, chugging tugs, and she loved like any schoolboy the excitement of the occasional ocean-going steamer that forced the Tower Bridge to raise its arms.

Herbert told her of the Navy, of his ship in particular, and of the gallant men who had sailed with him, for in the last year of the war he had been in command of a corvette, and he had loved both his ship and crew. Margaret found herself sad to think of this fine man who had commanded other men in a time of turmoil, working ignominiously as an insurance clerk, a nonentity in a crowded city, and she suggested to him that he should emigrate to a new country—Canada, perhaps, or Australia, where his native enterprise and resolution would be better appreciated. He looked at her strangely when she spoke in this way as if he were deeply moved. She was deeply moved herself, and she thought that her friend only needed sufficient encouragement to spur him on.

Sometimes, after they had eaten their sandwiches, they strolled along past the other clerks and typists eating picnic lunches, and Margaret had to giggle at the furtive way they slid their sandwiches from the rustling paper bags into their mouths, as if eating in public was a crime. "How very *English*!" Margaret said, and Herbert asked her if she had ever been abroad, and she told him, No, only India, which she hardly remembered; then Herbert smiled a quiet smile, and said that one day they might do travelling in foreign parts together. It was this sort of thing that made her feel all sunny inside, as if wonderful treats were in store for them both.

III

Herbert didn't buy himself a bike; instead he bought the Austin from his friend. Three or four evenings a week he would meet her under the clock at Victoria—for they never changed their rendezvous after that first encounter. As soon as Margaret got home from the office, tired and sticky after her ride through the fetid streets, she would bathe, and afterwards splash herself liberally with lavender water. She would eat supper—something very light like a salad, or some fresh fruit—sitting in her dressing-gown by the open window, the tray in her lap. She allowed herself plenty of time to get dressed, for she luxuriated in leisure after the heat of the day. Then cool and elegant in one of her new dresses, wearing her white hat with the floppy brim, her neat white shoes, and her white handbag, she would walk to the station. With Victoria their starting-point, almost any voyage became possible: they might travel to Brighton, to Paris, or even further, to places like Naples, or Venice. But for the time being, they were satisfied to stroll easily to the car, to drive out of the sultry city, where the air smelt like a bedroom slept in with the windows tight shut. Into the cool, leafy sweetness of the rambling country lanes they drove, with the windscreen, the windows and the sunshine roof wide open. Sometimes they went onwards till the light drained from the sky, till dusk and then darkness engulfed them, and the headlights picked out the bright eyes of cats as they flashed across the road. They talked or they were silent, as the mood took them, but always they seemed to be happy and in rhythm with one another.

They collected memories like snapshots, and snapshots also, for Herbert had an old Kodak that they took with them wherever they went. When they got the prints back from the chemist's at the back of the office, they rushed in high excitement to their lunch spot so that they could pore over them in peace, reliving the moments past and laughing in sheer delight because not only had they been happy, but they were happy, and, best of all, they had such an abundance of happiness to come.

For Margaret, the photographs were hardly necessary, for she kept a vivid store of tableaux and scenes far richer than the work of any camera. She saw them, for instance, sitting side by side on the wistaria-hung balcony of The Doves at Hammersmith. The river slid past, reflecting the bright lights of the city and a star or two that grew out of the soft sky. The other drinkers murmured quietly to each other in the background, and on her tongue was the cool, bitter-sweet taste of lemonade shandy. He was there by her side, silent, but entirely with her.

"Please God, let me hold this moment for ever and ever," she thought. "Whatever is to come—sickness, or loneliness, or old age and death—let it be defeated by such moments of companionship."

And Herbert, as so often, seemed to sense what she was thinking.

"You know, Margaret," he said softly, "we've had a great stroke of luck, you and I—haven't we?"

"Yes, Herbert," she whispered, "we have."

IV

There was the day they went punting from Cambridge to Granchester. Herbert was rather good with the pole, and they passed many a sweating undergraduate with apparent ease. They took tea at Granchester out of doors in a leafy orchard, the sun dappling the rich green grass. When it grew cooler, they re-embarked in the fragile craft for the journey back to the boathouse, and the car. Margaret, reclining languidly on the cushions whilst her fingers trailed in the cool water, wondered at Herbert's energy, and asked him if he wouldn't like her to take over for a bit.

"Stay where you are, lass," he commanded. "I may be a bit past me punting prime, but I've not yet got to the stage when I can sit back whilst a woman does the work. Besides, the current's doing most of it."

"Won't you be stiff tomorrow?" she asked.

"Happen I will," he said, "but it won't hurt. Look, Margaret, d'you see that dragon-fly? What a beauty, eh?"

He straightened his back, letting the pole glide on the water, and he turned to watch the big insect hovering over the bubbles of the wake. A shadow passed over Margaret—"Look out!" she screamed, "Herbert, look out!" But it was too late, and the punt had slid nearly its entire length under the low foot-bridge before he could duck. He grasped a section of scrolled ironwork with both hands as the deck slid from beneath him. For a few, agonizing seconds he hung from the bridge by his fingers, then, with a look of utter despair, he let himself drop into the dark water.

He was a good swimmer, easily regained the punt, and with her help hauled himself aboard. Dripping wet, with his red hair plastered over his forehead, he looked so doleful a spectacle that she could not restrain her laughter, and then he had to laugh, too.

"Your face . . ." she gasped, "your face . . . as you dropped!" Together they laughed till their sides ached.

"Oh, please stop," she said, "or I shall burst! Here, you must dry yourself." And she pulled from her white handbag a neatly folded handkerchief, the absurd inadequacy of which sent the pair of them into fresh gales of laughter.

V

One evening they went to the open-air theatre in Regent's Park to watch a performance of *The Tempest*. Both astonished by Shakespeare's power of enchantment, they watched Prospero's projects gathering to a head. The light drained from the sky, white lamps illuminated the actors, and behind them tall trees soared into the gathering dusk, the rustling leaves touched with red and blue. Prospero was speaking of his art:

> Ye elves of hills, brooks, standing lakes, and groves;
> And ye, that on the sand with printless foot
> Do chase the ebbing Neptune and do fly him
> When he comes back . . .

Margaret shuddered. How did Shakespeare know? How on earth did he know? Herbert put his raincoat over her shoulders, mistaking her emotion for cold, but she accepted his gesture quietly, with a nod of thanks for his thoughtfulness. It *was* getting a little chilly, in any case.

When the performance was over, they walked arm-in-arm across the little bridge spanning the boating lake, to Baker Street; and they found there a little restaurant whose lights were not too harsh, where they could drink a cup of coffee in peace.

They had both been moved to silence. Margaret was thinking that Prospero, at the last, had broken his magic staff, drowned his book, and released his lovely, delicate Ariel to the winds. This was only good and sensible, but she felt her throat tight with tears at so great a loss. Herbert seemed to understand completely, and they sipped the hot, sweet coffee without talking, happy in the comfort of each other's company.

VI

They went to Arundel, and took one of the blunt-nosed, walnut-shell rowing boats on the glassy lake. It was mid-afternoon, and the sun was very hot. Lazily, Herbert dipped the miniature oars in the water, and the sun turned the drops that fell from them into liquid gold. A great white swan glided up to them, and, involuntarily, she stiffened.

"It's all right, lass," Herbert said, "he only wants summat to eat. Give him that cucumber sandwich we left."

She took it from the haversack, broke it into pieces, and threw it into the water a few yards from the boat. Effortlessly, like a royal yacht, the white bird coursed to the spot, lowered his strong neck, gobbled the pieces of soaked bread, then slid back to Margaret, watching her with beady expectant eyes.

"I haven't any more left, swan," she said a little tremulously —"please go away and leave us."

The swan bowed his head in reply, circled the blunt prow, and headed for another boat in which were a fat, bald-headed man, sweating at the oars in shirt-sleeves and braces, and a plump, robin-redbreast woman in an orange dress and brown straw hat. They seemed overjoyed to have to entertain so royal a guest, and robin-redbreast rummaged in a large, brown-paper parcel for food.

"He understood me," whispered Margaret—"would you have believed it?"

Herbert laughed a superior, masculine laugh.

"Well, you must admit that he's got good manners, lass. It's breeding that counts every time—that's how you learn to be gracious."

"I can tell you this much," Margaret rejoined, "he never learnt to be as gracious as that in a girls' boarding-school."

VII

They were always laughing; in fact it seemed to both of them that they had never laughed so much in their lives.

One Saturday, they drove in an ambling sort of way in the direction of Pangbourne, with the intention of taking out a sailing dinghy on the Thames for an hour or two. They stopped at a pub, with green tables and chairs laid out under apple trees, for rolls, cheese, and beer, and afterwards they buzzed sleepily down a meandering country lane, each content to drift in his own thoughts, when all at once, they saw that they were passing a country fair.

Both of them woke up.

"Shall we see what it's like, lass?" asked Herbert.

"Oh, yes, do let's!" she answered, full of enthusiasm.

He parked the car in the shadow of an oak tree, and they walked, arm-in-arm, on a tour of inspection. There was a merry-go-round wheezing and thumping its own, special music; there were swing-boats, which the village lads tugged higher and higher, delighting in the shrieks of their girls who clutched hold of the guide-rope with one hand, and their billowing skirts with the other.

"Like a go?" Herbert asked, and Margaret's tummy turned over at the thought.

"No, thank you," she said. "It makes me sea-sick just to watch."

There were coconut-shies, rolling-penny tables, shooting-booths, a fat lady, a thin man, and a fortune-teller. The people looked different from Londoners: they had the solid, leisurely look of people who dine regularly on plenty of good, underdone roast beef and ale.

Margaret and Herbert paused by a stall of toffee-apples.

"Fair makes my mouth water," said Herbert; "let's muck in and have one."

"Yes, let's," Margaret agreed.

Herbert paid his shilling for them both, and handed Margaret the shiny, amber-encrusted fruit that made her mouth water.

They were being watched by a small boy of brown eyes, rosy cheeks, and dark curly hair. Herbert paused in the middle of a bite.

"Here, young fella," he said, "have a bite of mine!"

The child continued to stare, silently pleading.

"All right, lad, tha's won," said Herbert—"another toffee-apple if you please, Miss."

He squatted on his haunches to give it to the boy who took it without a word, never taking his eyes off Herbert's face.

"Na, then, young fella me lad, what's tha say?" he said.

There was silence.

"Say 'Thank you,'" said Margaret, bending down to him, and recalling Miss Pritchard with sudden vividness.

"'Ank you," the boy said, looking at Margaret, and suddenly licking the apple with the energy of a puppy.

They both laughed and went their way.

"Let's have a go on the merry-go-round," said Herbert.

They were shoved from behind, like a large dog, the little boy forced his way between them, still chewing, his face smeared with toffee.

"Let's take him with us," said Margaret.

"Right-o," said Herbert.

The prancing horses came circling slowly to a standstill. Herbert scooped up the boy in his arms, waited for Margaret to settle herself astride a magnificent white charger with flaring nostrils then handed the child to her to hold in her lap. He himself climbed on to the tall dappled grey on the outside like a knight-errant protecting his charges.

The attendant in blue overalls took the money, the two horses began rising and falling, the organ wheezed, and Herbert, suddenly intoxicated with the excitement of the fair, began singing, very loud, and very flat:

He flew through . . . the air with . . . the greatest of ease,
The daring . . . young man on . . . the flying trapeze,
His movements . . . were graceful . . . and certain to please,
And my heart . . . was stolen . . . away . . .

The faces watching them, the tents of the side-shows, trees, blue sky and cotton-wool clouds, began blurring into one another like a water-colour that the water has spilled over. The horses plunged and rose, and Margaret, clinging tightly to the little boy lest he should fall, began to be sorry that she had eaten a toffee-apple so soon after drinking beer; but the little boy laughed joyously, in sheer, animal delight.

Not a moment too soon for Margaret, the roundabout slowed. Herbert swung off his horse, took the child from her, and helped her to climb thankfully back to solid earth.

A woman in a blue uniform with white cuffs came running up to them, very flustered.

"Oh, there you are, David! You naughty little boy, what have you been up to?"

Margaret astonished herself by intervening with complete equanimity—and how astonished would Miss Pritchard have been!

"I hope you don't mind, we took him on the merry-go-round with us."

"How very kind," said the nurse, "how very kind indeed. He is such a terror, you know, he ran off and left me before I could say a word. I'm sorry he bothered you . . ."

"No bother at all, Ma'm," Herbert said. "He gave us a great time."

"Well, thank you again," said the nurse, and moved off with a guilty briskness, dragging the child by the arm.

"What a proper nincompoop," exclaimed Herbert. "Fancy letting the kid run off, and then blaming him for naughtiness! I bet she was having her fortune told, too."

"I know," said Margaret, "and he was such a dear little fellow. I had a governess like that once, and I hated her."

"No wonder," said Herbert; "I'd just as soon have a drunken father as a fool like that."

They both laughed, but none too heartily. They both felt a little flat, though neither of them could have said quite why. The sun continued to shine, the fair was as jolly as ever—but now the jollity seemed garish, and the thumping music and the bustling crowds weighed on them like a coming storm.

"Come on, lass," Herbert muttered, "I've had enough of this place."

So that particular souvenir was slightly tinged with inexplicable melancholy; but a photograph is nonetheless nostalgic for being slightly dark.

Chapter Six

I

On the last Friday in June, Herbert went off to take his two week's summer holiday at Butlin's Holiday Camp at Skegness where he had booked the year before. Herbert had tried to change his two weeks to the beginning of September when Margaret was due for hers, but at Boothby's, holidays were staggered, and it was difficult to alter the vacation rota without drawing a great deal of attention, and causing a lot of fuss. He decided, with her approval, to leave the arrangement as it was.

His train left Liverpool Street at 5.40, and Margaret, having for once succeeded in getting Gladys Peach to pay her back and stand in for her for the last thirty minutes, left early to see him off. He found a corner seat facing the engine, and reserved it with his old navy raincoat; he placed his canvas holdall and tennis racket on the rack; he walked with her to the bookstall where he bought himself the *Evening Standard* and a paper-backed detective story for the journey. All this still left him ten full minutes, most of which he spent leaning out of the carriage window, and staring at Margaret.

"I hope you get some decent weather and plenty of tennis," said Margaret.

"What's that?" he shouted back.

"I hope you get decent weather for tennis," Margaret shouted—there was a great hissing of steam which made conversation difficult.

"Thanks very much," he shouted, "I hope you get in some cycling."

"Thanks," she called, "perhaps I'll cycle up to Skegness to see you next week-end."

"What's that? Come again, lass!"

"I said I'll cycle up to Skegness next week-end," she shouted, "but I was joking."

"Oh, that's a pity," he said.

They stared at one another for a while, Margaret searching her mind for some topic of conversation. A fat lady in a brown dress, trying to control three bursting attaché cases and a crammed paper carrier-bag, was almost a welcome break to the strain: she took quite three minutes to get herself settled, and Herbert, always the gentleman, arranged all her belongings on the rack for her. When he got back to the window, the guard was blowing his whistle. Herbert was red in the face from his exertions.

"Margaret, lass, write to me," he shouted, and the train jerked and was off.

"Righty-o," she called back. "Have a good time."

"Margaret, I'll write every day if you will."

"Yes, all right—'bye, 'bye..."

He shouted something that sounded like "God speed," but he was too far away for her to be sure. He waved furiously and was still waving when the train coiled to the left, and he was out of sight.

She sighed, and was surprised to find a lump in her throat. As a matter of fact, the last few minutes had been a strain, and it was a relief to be left alone; but she felt just a wee bit hot in the eyes—probably because saying goodbye on stations made her think of going off to school leaving Daddy on the platform, and even more of waving good-bye to Daddy, knowing she was not going to see him for years and years, as the boat-train bore him to the P. & O. that was taking him to India—perhaps for good.

She blew her nose on her handkerchief, and walked briskly to the station buffet, where she got herself an egg sandwich wrapped in cellophane, and a good, strong cup of tea. The trouble with her was she needed nourishment—at lunch-time she hadn't been very hungry, and hadn't eaten very much.

II

She sat in her armchair in her dressing-gown, cool after her bath, and enjoying the freshness of lavender water. She had opened the windows wide, drawing up her chair to them, so that the faint breeze fanned her forehead. For a while she looked over the roofs and castellated chimneys of the houses opposite, to the softening evening sky. She focused her eyes on the pad of writing paper in her lap, and began to write.

Dear Herbert:

I promised to write to you every day, and as you see I mean to keep my promise. It was beastly saying good-bye at Liverpool Street, because of the noise and rush and everything, but I'm glad I saw you off just the same. It's horrid waving good-bye on station platforms, but it's worse when there's no one to wave good-bye to. That, we both know, from experience.

Well, I must say it's rather funny to be sitting here in my dressing-gown, knowing that all I'll get dressed for is to run this to the letter-box. Perhaps I'll go for a walk to the river, and get a breath of fresh air. But I shall miss meeting you under the clock as usual, and I shall miss the Austin.

It occurs to me that this has been a lovely summer, the happiest that I have ever spent! I have you to thank for it. I very much look forward to your return; in fact, I've just this moment decided to paint my room and change the furniture around a bit, and when you come back I shall have you to supper. Meanwhile, have a very good holiday, and be careful not to drown when you go swimming, or catch pneumonia.

Yours sincerely,
Margaret.

She addressed the envelope, folded up the letter without rereading it, stuck down the flap, and went to the desk for a stamp. She had a nice, warm feeling that she had written rather well, and with sincerity. Yet she was not entirely sorry to be by herself again for a while. She could reorganise her room—as she had written to Herbert that she would—and get her thoughts in order. These past weeks she had let everything go hang: her mind felt like a chest o' drawers full of underclothes that needed sorting. Over the next fortnight she would go for long cycle rides by herself, repaint her room: grey and lemon, perhaps—a warm dove-grey; and keep the armchair permanently by the window, and pull the oak table into the middle of the room, so that two could sit at it in comfort.

Her plans filled her with enthusiasm and energy, and on an impulse she decided that she would post Herbert's letter and go for a cycle ride. It would give her something to write about to Herbert tomorrow. Wouldn't it be a nice idea to keep a journal of her doings? But that was a brainwave! She would fill it in each night before she went to bed. Not only would she have something for Herbert, but she would help herself to untangle her thoughts.

III

Saturday, June 28th. 8.17 p.m., (she wrote).
I'm sitting on Parliament Hill, all London at my feet. From this bench the grass slopes down to Parliament Hill Fields, where several games of cricket are being played. Beyond the foot of the hills is Kentish Town (presumably, where the cricketers come from, for these are not Lords players in immaculate white, but scraggy youths and shrill voiced girls, drab as London sparrows). Beyond Kentish Town is the smoke-haze, I suppose of King's Cross, from which new blocks of flats (Council?) rise like great ships.

Then there is a great sea of roofs spreading as far as I can see, and from this sea rise spires and factory chimneys, like the funnels of ocean liners; and a little to the left is St Paul's, which is like the dome of a royal palace built on an enchanted island; and the evening sky is blue, white, gold, fiery red, and purple. (I wax poetic!)

Spent the morning doing housework: doing laundry at the launderette, cleaning the stove, and polishing the furniture. Tomorrow I shall begin painting walls. I decided on pearly grey for the fireplace wall and the bed wall, and lemon yellow for the wardrobe wall and the window wall. These colours will match the curtains. I'll keep the oak table oak even if it doesn't quite match, but I'm thinking of lacquering the wardrobe white.

A postcard from H.B. arrived at noon. A hideous picture of Butlin's swimming pool absolutely crawling with gaudy bathers (it reminded me of nothing so much as the advertisements for Campbell's Vegetable Soup!). Poor dear, he's quite without taste in these things, and I can just imagine his water-colours of ships that he painted in the navy! But I don't mind: he's very sincere, and all the people who would sneer at him for lack of polish or imagination aren't worth a button.

He'd written as soon as he arrived last night: *I miss you, though it all looks very nice, and the chalet is clean and comfortable. I wish you were here. Yours, Herbert.*

I wish I was there, too, in a way, though I think Butlin's must be simply frightful! No, on second thoughts, it's nice to be home on my own for a little—I haven't been by myself for weeks, and really I need to be. It'll be very nice when he comes back, and I'm going to have him to supper that Sunday. I've already written inviting him.

IV

Sunday, June 29th. 10.30 p.m.

Spent the morning painting walls, and finished them before lunch (these rubber-base paints that you put on with a roller are amazing!). The room looks strange, but I think very nice and exciting. Afterwards I wanted to get out of the smell (which actually wasn't too bad) and I cycled to Lyon's Corner House at Marble Arch for lunch (steak and chips, with peas and grilled tomatoes; and to follow, trifle, ice-cream, and coffee: 4/9d. a bit extravagant but worth it!

Afterwards I cycled to Regent's Park, and sat in a deck-chair in the Queen Alexandra Rose Garden. (I was so exhausted it just wasn't true, and I slept for nearly two hours!) Then I wrote to Herbert to tell him about the grey and lemon walls, and went and had tea in the cafeteria (very crowded and messy). Then I went to see a bad film at the Victoria Palace—a Western with lots of shooting, and fighting, and those frightful chorus girls that droop around in black lace and eyelashes, and blow smoke through their nostrils as if they were dragons! There were some nice horses (which is why I went) and it was lovely to see them galloping, proud and splendid. Much more real than the rest of the story!

I'm sitting in bed writing this, for I'm going to have an early night after all my exertions. It's very peaceful and quiet; the moths flap round the lamp, and throw dancing shadows on the ceiling.

I wish Herbert were going to be at the office tomorrow; it will be horrid without him. Good night, Margaret, sweet dreams.

V

But in spite of all the activity she had planned for herself, and in spite of the journal—which was a good deal of fun—the week dragged. At lunch-time she went to the Tower Gardens as before, but the newspaper or woman's magazine she took with her was no substitute for Herbert's gruff, Yorkshire voice, and watching the tugs chug past was not much fun without his stories.

He wrote to her at the office every day, with great discretion printing her name and address so that no one would know about their friendship, a wise move, for she had no wish to become a subject for office gossip. His letters were nice, but rather formal: he'd met an old shipmate of his, now married to a Yorkshire girl, who had a bit too much weight on her, and a bit too much to say for herself; but there were two fine lads to whom he was teaching cricket. The weather was fine, and so on. The food was all right, and there was plenty of it. And in every letter, he wished that she was with him, which was perhaps just a cliché, but knowing how sincere he was, she felt that he must mean it.

Time hung on her most heavily in the evenings. She bathed and ate a light supper just as before; then she wrote to him—not long letters, which would never do, but short, cheerful ones, telling him about her doings, and the doings at the office. Then she went for long walks, for cycling seemed to need too much work and the weather was really too hot. After her bath it was pleasant to wear her cool dress and white shoes, and stroll to Hyde Park or Green Park with her sketching block, and sit in a deck chair for an hour or two till dusk fell, watching the effects of light on the trees; it was charming to watch the young lovers sauntering by, or reclining on the grass.

Monday, Tuesday, Wednesday, Thursday, Friday. Life had slowed down to its wonted pace, and she found herself counting the days to Sunday week when he was due to return. She decided she would have a special little party for him—roast beef and Yorkshire pudding, made in the Yorkshire way, of course, and served as he'd told her his mother had served it, before the meat with good gravy; and afterwards, home-made apple pie and ice-cream. She might even run to a bottle of wine.

How different life was now that she had someone who cared whether she lived or died, for whom she cared! True, the time dragged while he was away, but she had so much to look forward to when he got back. They would go into the country again at week-ends, and take long drives in the Austin, and perhaps they could play tennis in the park. Autumn would be such fun to share, for the colours were beautiful, and walking through the golden groves of autumn leaves, breathing the melancholy, autumn air would be delightful.

Winter was not something to be dreaded, now. They would have lovely, cosy evenings in front of the gas-fire, with delicious, cosy suppers. She would sit and sew, or knit, or they would both paint—she could certainly show him a thing or two about water-colours! They would chat, and talk of the summer's doings, and they would look over the snapshots they had taken. Christmas would be such fun, too! She would roast a turkey, and give him a pair of gloves and a muffler. What's more, she would knit them herself.

She recalled very vividly that night that she had resolved to make friends with people. Then it had seemed impossible, and suddenly it had become easy. Now her whole life was different. The girls at the office would say that she had been a frustrated spinster, and only wanting a man, and so on, and they would get completely the wrong idea of her happiness. Herbert and she were companions. There was nothing ugly involved at all, and this companionship seemed like the most beautiful thing she had ever had. She wanted to give Herbert everything that he hadn't had since his mother died. She wanted to make up to him all that he had suffered from his marriage with that terrible and cruel woman. She wanted to encourage him in his ambitions, and she felt very strongly that it was her mission to make him a great success in his own eyes.

VI

Friday was very hot and uncomfortable. There had been no letter from Herbert in the morning, which was both a disappointment and a worry, and the chattering of the typists' room got so much on her nerves that she wanted to scream.

At the lunch hour the Tower Gardens were crowded and she could find no seat. In the end, she sat on the base of a great black cannon used at Waterloo. She tried to ignore the shrill, grubby little boys playing soldiers and stared across the shimmering river at a ship being loaded at the wharf opposite. She thought how lovely it would be to sail with her, out of the heat and dust of sun-scorched London, to the cool, sea breezes! How lovely it would be to get away from town for a while and bathe in cool water, as she had as a child, and run along the beach with nothing on but a bathing costume, and dig a great sand castle, and go shrimping. Perhaps she should really go to Skegness for the week-end—surprise Herbert by turning up there tonight, on the 5.40 from Liverpool Street.

But there would probably be difficulty about finding her accommodation at such short notice, and to have to start looking for a room at midnight after the train got in would be no fun at all. Besides, Herbert might have made all sorts of arrangements with his friends, and she would be nothing but a nuisance. No, she had better go to Cambridge, or somewhere, on her bike, and wait for next week-end with such patience as she could muster.

When she returned to the office, there was a telegram on her typewriter—Herbert! He had drowned himself! She tore it open:

MEET ME TEA-SHOP STORRINGTON SATURDAY NOON ALL WELL WILL EXPLAIN THEN NOTHING TO WORRY ABOUT ONLY SUDDEN DECISION   LOVE HERBERT

Chapter Seven

I

The green bus that she had taken from Worthing left her in Storrington Market Square with a puff of exhaust smoke and hot dust. It was fifteen minutes to noon and very hot: she took her still-folded hanky, lavender-scented, from her white bag to pat her forehead. She was wearing a new, poppy-coloured silk dress that she'd bought on Friday afternoon, having left the office an hour early to rush to the Oxford Street shops. She felt that she looked rather nice.

With her head slightly bowed under her shady white hat, for the sun was beating down, she walked slowly towards the little tea-room. As she got nearer, two or three butterflies began fluttering in her tummy. They grew larger and more violent. Why had Herbert wired to her to meet him a week early? Why had he left Skegness without finishing his holiday? Well, he had told her not to worry, and in just fifteen minutes she would know. Didn't she have any idea? Yes, she had an idea, but she didn't want to mention it . . .

Her mouth had gone very dry, and she was suddenly breathless. It was very silly to get so agitated: very silly indeed! It wasn't as if she was being taken to see the Headmistress for the first time, knowing very well that she was going to be asked about Bradshaw. "Bradshaw's only a game very little girls play," the Head had said, and Margaret had felt sick. But Herbert would never say that.

She wasn't afraid that Herbert would ask her about Bradshaw, was she? She wouldn't answer him if he did. She would say, "That's just a private secret, and I can't tell you anything. I mustn't tell you anything—it would be wicked . . ."

The Austin was parked outside the cottage! She wanted to walk away before he saw her. But what a juggins she would be if she did! If she went back home there would only be her empty room, and then she *would* be sorry. No, she must be a good soldier and advance.

The tea-room with its polished oak tables and chairs was cool and deserted; but, through the open casement, she saw the back of his head, his reddish hair thinning on top and his ears pink— he was sitting in the garden. A giggle bubbled in her throat, but she swallowed it; instead she tiptoed to the window, put her hand through the opening, and gently tweaked his left ear.

"Boo!" she said.

"Margaret!" he exclaimed, slewing round in his chair. "You're early, as usual."

"You're looking very well—you've gone and caught the sun."

"You mean the sun caught me! I feel like a beetroot and I'm peeling like an onion! 'Come into the garden, Maud,' and let's have a bite of lunch . . ."

He stood up for her as she walked across the crazy paving to the table, which stood under a brightly coloured parasol. He was wearing a dark-blue silk scarf with wavy lines—R.N.V.R., of course; a snowy-white shirt open at the collar; a navy blazer with brass buttons, and cream flannels superbly creased.

"Herbert Bacon," she said, "you look as if you're captaining the Royal yacht at Cowes. I've never seen such a dandy."

"You don't look so dusty yourself," he said, offering her a grass-green garden chair. The circular table was set with a white cloth, and in the centre there was a little blue jug of snap-dragons, velvety-red, lemon-yellow, and rust. The parasol above was segmented blue, yellow, green and red.

"How very pretty it all is," Margaret said. "It looks like an advertisement for the South of France! Now, tell me, Herbert, why have you left Skegness a week early."

"Can't you guess, lass?"

"Did you . . .? Did you dislike it there?"

"Aye, that I did."

"Why was that? Was the food bad?"

"No, that was all right. The grub wasn't the reason. Guess again."

"You didn't like the noise!"

"No, I didn't at that; but that's not the reason either. Guess again."

Her tummy turned over and her head began to spin as if she were on a merry-go-round.

"You didn't like the people!" she managed to say.

"Not much. But that's still not the real reason. Guess once more, Margaret Finlay."

"No!" she said desperately. "No, no! I can't guess anymore."

"Can't you, Margaret Finlay. You ought, you know, because point of fact it's you."

"No, not me. It isn't me."

"It isn't me!" he echoed, in a falsetto imitation of her. "It is you, I tell you. I love you, Margaret Finlay, and I want you to marry me. And if you didn't guess that much, well, all I can say is you must be a nincompoop."

The parasol whirled like a cartwheel, and she gripped her seat with both hands lest she should fly off into space like a meteor! She felt deadly sick.

"Here, lass, I'm sorry—I'd no idea it would be such a shock to you, or I wouldn't have been so blunt. Have a glass of water—

here, swallow down this."

Her hand was so shaking that she spilled the water over the cloth; but Herbert stood up and held the glass to her chattering teeth: she was able to take two or three sips.

"I'm very sorry to have upset you, lass; I thought you'd have guessed from my wire. Didn't you?"

"No," she shuddered; "no, I didn't guess."

"Well, take it easy, lass. Don't say *No* just because you're surprised. Think it over till after lunch, eh?"

His voice seemed to come from down an immensely long tunnel, but she nodded. It was the quickest way of ending discussion. She wanted time—time to think. Herbert Bacon wanted her to be his wife—would you believe it?

She remembered Daddy, singing as he shaved:

>Monday, Tuesday, Wednesday, Thursday,
>May be merry and bright!
>But I'm going to be married on Sunday
>And now it is Saturday night!

The church was crowded to capacity; round the altar were great wreaths of while lilies; the organ boomed. The congregation rose—"It's her! It's the bride!—Isn't she just beautiful! Like a princess!" The tall figure in white proceeded down the aisle on the arm of her still taller, moustached and distinguished-looking father. She was heavily veiled, and she carried a great bouquet of white lilies.

"Here comes the bride, all dressed in white . . ."

They reached the altar, and she was aware of another by her side—one whom she dared not look at—and the priest was intoning: "If any man can show just cause, why they may not lawfully be joined together, let him now speak, or else hereafter for ever hold his peace."

The witch-woman was going to protest! The game was up!

"I've never heard such nonsense, *she* can't be married! She's Margaret Finlay! Margaret Finlay can never be married: Margaret Finlay is cursed!"

"You're the most evil woman in the world, and I hate you," Margaret cried. "You're the witch! You're the snake-woman! You're poisoned with evil to your very heart! Daddy, don't listen to her—she is the traitress who has blighted all your kingdom, and it's from her spell that you are dying: but Bradshaw and I have found the flower to cure you. We must free the kingdom from the blight, Daddy; we must free the kingdom from the blight and destroy the witch and her evil for ever."

"Margaret, Margaret, wake up. Lunch is on the table! Margaret, listen to me . . ."

"I can hear you. It's all right, I was only day-dreaming. Why, Herbert, you've gone quite pale! Are you too much in the sun? Get under the shade of the parasol, my dear. Why, what a lovely lunch your Yorkshire friend has brought! Ham, salad, and brown bread and butter—delicious! I'm absolutely famished after all that agitation! Why, Herbert, what's all this? *Wine!*"

"Well, lass, it's not every day I propose marriage," he said complacently.

"No. No, of course not."

"You can't give me your answer, yet, can you, lass? I'm a bit impatient to know . . ."

"I . . . I don't know, Herbert. I don't know what to say . . . I *really* don't know . . ."

"Well, wait a while, lass, and eat your lunch first—you can't decide these things on an empty stomach."

"No. No, of course not."

II

How *good* food was when you were hungry! It didn't have to be elaborate by any means: just good, simple, and nourishing, the homely fare that has nourished Englishmen for generations. Firm, pink ham, pale veined and thinly sliced, with a flavour at once delicate and positive! Fresh brown bread and farm-house butter! Crisp, yellow hearts of lettuce! And if the sunlight can glitter through a glass of chilled white wine . . .

"Herbert, the wine is excellent! *Bon Appétit!*" as they say in France.

"The same to you, Margaret. Lass, you know, what I want to say about us, Margaret lass—I mean about us getting married . . ."

"Excuse me interrupting you, Herbert my dear, but the French have a saying—I'm perfectly sure—about not spoiling a good meal with discussion. Save all that for later. We'll go for a walk after lunch, then you can bring it up again. Oh, fresh raspberries and cream! How absolutely scrumptious! I shall make an absolute pig of myself, I know . . ."

III

"If you've finished with your coffee, lass, let's call for the bill and go for a little walk."

"All right, Herbert. Let's climb to the top of the downs again."

"Don't you think it's a bit too hot for that, lass?"

"Of course not. It'll be simply too good to be true on top of the hill, and we'll get a lovely sea breeze."

"Can't we just stroll down the lane, lass? I do want to do a bit of talking . . ."

"You can save that till we reach the highest summit. You have to earn blessings, you know."

"I'm . . . I'm not sure I know what you mean, lass."

"You'll see."

IV

Climbing the sacred mountain to find the purple flower—he was panting like an old donkey-engine. "Be of good courage, and we will yet triumph over the snake-woman and all her evil works."

"What's that, you say!"

"I was just muttering to myself. You're a bit out of condition, Herbert Bacon. You should have bought yourself that bicycle."

"Aye, I should. I would have done, too, if I'd known you were going to make me climb Everest!"

V

They arrived at the base of the circle of trees that topped the hill.

"Let's sit here," she said—be it admitted, somewhat out of breath herself, and no doubt of a similar shade of poppy to her dress. She was perspiring freely, but oh, she felt so good! Herbert was rather pale, and he gasped for air.

"Sit you down, dear-heart, and take a good, long rest," she said, and she squatted, hugging her knees—had she known they were going to climb mountains, she would have worn clothes more suitable.

"Why, Herbert," she exclaimed, "this is just where we had our picnic when we came in the spring—I'm sure I remember that gorse bush! Do you remember how we played hide-and-seek!"

"Aye, that I do," said Herbert—he sounded thoroughly worn

out. "Here, lass, wouldn't you like my blazer to sit on?"

"Certainly not. Why should I dirty your blazer?"

"But it'd be a pity to muss that dress—you look a fair treat in it, lass.'"

"Thank you," she said, "but I won't muss it, I promise. The grass is bone dry. It needs rain badly, doesn't it? Everything looks so *dry* . . ."

"Margaret, lass, don't let's talk of the weather . . ."

"No," she said slowly. "No, don't let's—let's play hide-and-seek instead!"

"Margaret, please don't tease me. You've got a grand sense of fun, I know, and I'm a bit of a wet blanket about these things: I'm sorry, but I've too much on my mind for jokes—no, don't interrupt again, please, lass. I don't want you to rush your decision, or anything, but I do want to argue my case as best I can. I know I'm not much of a chap: I was brought up in a slum, and my father was a drunk, and I went and made a proper mess of my first marriage. I know you're a lady born, with twice the education I've had, I know you're ten years younger than me at least, and I know I'm nothing but a miserable insurance clerk. You've every reason for turning me down; but I don't know as you'd be right if you did.

"Before we got to know each other we were both of us pretty lonely, weren't we? Leastwise I was! And since we've had each other's company, we've had some grand times, haven't we? We get on well with each other, we like the same things, and even though we come from totally different backgrounds, we have pretty much the same values—haven't we, lass?"

"Yes, I suppose we have, really."

The flies were worrying her. In spite of the sea breeze, there were lots of flies and bugs around. A great fat fly was crawling up her calf. She watched it, fascinated and revolted; and she slapped at it, hoping to squash it quick; but she missed. She wished she had a tail to flick at the beastly things . . .

"Are you listening, Margaret?"

"Yes, I'm listening. Aren't these flies a bore, though?"

"Margaret, lass, what do we have to look forward to without each other? A lonely, selfish old age, probably with no friends that amount to anything—neither of us seems to be much good at making friends—do we? Neither of us have much of a family, and neither of us have any place we can really call home. At least together we've got companionship. And you're a young healthy woman—there's no reason on earth why we shouldn't have a family! Somewhere down I've got some guts left, you know, if only I had summat to work for like a wife and kids . . ."

Married, she would have to be with him all the time. She would have to cook for him, wash up dishes after every meal, and at night hear him breathing in the next, possibly even in the same bed. Why did people always demand more and more of you? They could never be satisfied with what you had to give them; they had to have more and more of your most cherished privacy; they tore off your clothes piece by piece until you were quite naked, until there was nothing more that you could call your own. Did they have to possess the whole? Wasn't it enough the part you gave them voluntarily?

". . . Margaret, I say why don't you answer me? Are you all right?"

"Of course I'm all right. What were you saying?"

"Together we could do such splendid things, lass. I've had this plan in my head for some time to emigrate to Australia, or perhaps Canada, and aim to set up my own business. I've got lots of ideas, you know; I'm not bad at figures, and I've never been afraid of hard work. Two old shipmates of mine have done it already—working to begin with in any old job that was going, looking at the lie of the land, and meanwhile saving a bit of capital for the right moment to start summat of their own. Now they've both got first rate businesses, the one in real estate in Toronto, and the other in women's clothes in Vancouver. I've half a mind to try for a job out there as office manager; but if I couldn't get it, I'd take anything, even manual labour if it gave me money to put by. Eventually, perhaps, I'd start a little restaurant business—I've always been interested in cooking, you know, and I know you are. Wouldn't it be fun to travel to foreign parts together, and begin a little English tea-shop in Canada or Australia? Think of getting the place ready, and furnishing it!—Just think of that. And perhaps later on we could go in for selling antiques and such like, on the side."

It all sounded very nice, but impossible, like a wild romance. A long sea voyage to the New World; a strange city; people with strange, filmic lives, driving huge cars like gangsters at terrifying speeds, and buying refrigerators as if they were mere frying-pans, and all the time chewing gum. In the middle of this, she and Herbert would establish a little bit of old England, a tea-shop with polished oak furniture, bits of brass on the walls, and English china on which they would serve hot buttered toast, tea-cakes, and muffins, scones with strawberry jam, and Devonshire cream. She would learn how to make ginger-nuts, parkin, and seed-cake.

It was a lunatic idea, to be sure, but it did sound exciting! Perhaps it wasn't so impossible. She had a little money that Gran had left her, and that, with her savings, might be a help if they were going to start something. Herbert was a hard worker, and very efficient—he certainly wasn't an up-in-the-air sort, to go in for wild schemes that were hopelessly impractical. After all, hadn't he risen from the lower decks in the war? A man who'd had none of the advantages of privileged education, to finish in command of his own ship . . .

"So someone at last wants to marry you. Do you really believe you would make him an adequate wife?" Mummy, reclining like a cat on the sofa, and jeering. "He's not had many . . . advantages, one might say—has he? One might say—mightn't one?—that he's a wee bit of a *yob*!" Mummy was a witch! "You're just a beastly snob; and in any case you haven't much to boast about—Gran always thought Daddy was marrying below himself!" "All right, Margaret, my poppet, may I ask what right you have even to think of marrying anybody? You're just a child!" "I'm not a child, I'm thirty-one!" "You're a child in the only way it really counts. Men have their . . . their needs, you know. Can you see yourself . . . *sharing a bed* with your little friend?" "I could get used to it—surely I could get used to it. If you loved someone enough you could learn to accept . . . even that!" "Don't be a little fool, Margaret Finlay . . ."

"Herbert, did you say something?"

"Aye, that I did: three times. I said give you a penny for them. What in heaven's name were you thinking of? You looked as if you'd seen a ghost, all pop-eyed and all!"

"I was just thinking . . . of your question, that's all."

"Well, I don't want to rush you, Margaret, but I do wish you'd consent to give me a fair trial at making you happy. I'm certain we could make a go of it! You know, this summer has been just great as far as I'm concerned. You're so much the sort of girl I really need! When I was a youngster, I had my head full of film-star rubbish—point of fact that's how I came to marry Violet. But I'll never make that mistake again! In a way, she did me good—if nothing else I've learnt that marrying, like everything else worth-while, is damned hard work, and that all the stories you hear about people living happy-ever-after are so much rubbish. When I married Vi I was marrying a young lad's pin-up girl, but I'm older now. I'll work hard for you, Margaret, I swear I will! I love you, Margaret, as a companion; I love being with you, and what's more, I love you as a woman and I want you."

The sun pressed down on the valley, and the air shimmered. In the distance a glass roof flashed white fire. "Pity the poor, wilting tomatoes," she thought, for it could only be a greenhouse. It was strange that such an expanse of glass didn't crack under the heat!

From the right a plume of white smoke spouted from the head of a long, black train that snaked across the valley towards Storrington. There was something terrible and inexorable about its rapid progress: so life took you from children's games in the garden to the serious business of living; and so it would take you, terribly, pitilessly, to old age, and finally death. Hadn't just that happened to Gran? The fine, tall, active, beautiful lady withering in the space of a few months into a toothless, babbling old crone. Such a little while ago, Gran had strode vigorously to the Park, Margaret holding her hand, and skipping and jumping round her as if she were a maypole. Now Gran was rotting flesh and decaying bone in a wooden box under ten feet of London clay. And Margaret? Margaret was thirty-two next birthday, and still playing children's games. Couldn't the dead bury their dead?

"What did tha' say, lass?"

"Oh, I'm sorry, I was just thinking out loud again."

"Sorry to have disturbed you, lass. I know you have things to think out, but I just don't want you to drift too far away from me, that's all."

"I suppose we all have to grow up and leave all that's gone before."

"Aye, lass, that's the way of it. I learnt that when I buried my mother..."

That train was bearing a coffin to its last resting-place. It was pulling into Storrington Station with a squeal of brakes, a series of jerks, and steam hissing from the wheels. Four pall-bearers, all in black, hoisted the heavy oaken box on to their shoulders. They knelt for M., who, dressed in shining white, covered the coffin with a shroud of rich velvet, black as midnight. At the head she placed a great horseshoe wreath of snow-white lilies, which transformed the sooty air of the little station with their sweet breath. They marched down the platform, through the sand-coloured hall of the ticket office, and out into the street. In slow time, they paced towards the church, followed only by M. in her white robes.

"Let the drums sound! Let the bagpipes play!" ordered M., for this was to be a warrior's funeral—*he* had always loved music.

> Ride a cock horse to Banbury Cross
> To see a fine lady upon a white horse . . .

The familiar tune, strangely wailing in slow time from the pipe band, brought the tears into her eyes: but a soldier's wife never showed grief in public. *He* would have wished her not to cry, but to accept the bereavement as inevitable, and to move on to new pastures without useless grief. The wishes he was no longer able to voice, she must respect. The cortège turned into the churchyard. From the west door came the priests in their vestments of white and black. Now the drums were hushed, the pipers silent . . .

> I am the resurrection and the life, saith the Lord: he that believeth in me, though he were dead, yet shall he live: and whosoever liveth and believeth in me, shall never die . . .

The coffin was lowered into the deep pit. M. closed her eyes tight, for her last farewell:

"Good-bye, dear-heart: God bless you . . ."

Something warm and wet on her neck!—She jerked round with a terrible shock: it was Herbert—he'd gone mad!

"Na then, lass," he grunted, and pushed her to the ground, staring at her with bulging, bloodshot eyes. Panic, utter panic seized her as he pressed his hot, wet, animal mouth against hers—she couldn't breathe! He struggled to possess her, tearing off her hat, her glasses, her clothes. He was a sex-maniac! This was the end!

Desperation gave her superhuman strength. She punched him in the throat, clawed at his face with her nails, and finally gave him a great push that flung him into the gorse bush. She was sobbing with anger and terror, but she had won! For once in her life she had fought the bully and had emerged the victor. He wouldn't dare to try anything now—she would kick him if he did! She found her glasses in the grass and put them on.

"Why... why ever did you do that?" he gasped. "I wasn't... I wasn't minded to do anything but kiss you. You..." he broke off, shaking his head. He had gone the colour of ashes. She could see that he was near crying. Well, it served him right for doing such a dreadful thing! But she wasn't one to kick a man when he was down: she turned away from him to stare down into the valley, and give him a chance to recover himself. She had to have time herself—so nearly had she made a most shocking mistake!

With several yards between them, they crouched on the hillside in the sweltering sun for fully forty-five minutes. They neither spoke nor moved. The birds sang, the crickets whirred, and from time to time trains down in the valley snorted and clanked. She didn't care how long he kept silent: the longer the better as far as she was concerned. She felt numb!

At length, from out the corner of her eyes, she saw him glance, first at his watch and then at her.

"Please say summat," he said. "Tell me off if you like, but say summat. Don't just hate me in silence."

She made no motion of having heard him.

"Margaret, lass," he begged, "don't get me wrong. I didn't mean to do anything but kiss you. Don't be so . . . so upset! You make me feel downright bad, as if I was going to rape you! You know I'd never do a thing like that, don't you now?"

She tried to answer politely, she tried very hard; but what could she possibly say?

She was saved by the piercing blast of a guide whistle. They both looked round: there was the guide mistress again, surrounded with her troop.

"Now girls," she said, "this afternoon you're going on a nature patrol to observe birds, insects, flowers and trees, and all the wild life there is to be found in this wood and its surroundings . . ."

Margaret found her voice:

"I think we'd better go down now," she said. "We must be getting back home, mustn't we?' She put on her hat and picked herself up, brushing the bits from her dress. He picked up his blazer, shook it, and followed her down the path at about five yards distance.

When they reached the road, he caught her up.

"Well, lass, what's your answer?" he asked.

"Answer? What answer?"

"Your answer to my question: will you marry me, Margaret Finlay?"

She thought of him panting and grunting on top of her; she smelled the dank smell of his breath; she saw his mottled skin, peeling like grated cheese on the red nose and forehead, and the large pores that were like the skin of an old grapefruit. She saw the little tufts of ginger hair that protruded from his nostrils and ears; she felt once again those hot, animal kisses. She shuddered.

They were nearly at the tea-room before she could trust herself to speak.

"Thank you for asking me," she said. "It's kind of you but I'm afraid I must refuse. You see—I suppose I should have mentioned it before—I am already engaged."

"Already engaged!" he echoed, horrified and incredulous.

"Yes, to one of my oldest friends, Pony Bradshaw. We live together, you know."

"Oh, God," he muttered, "and I never believed that story was true! I thought you'd made the whole thing up for the typists' room!"

"Made it up!" she exclaimed, "why, dear me, no: Bradshaw's more than real."

"But you've spent the whole summer with me!"

"Yes, I know. Bradshaw's been away—in Canada as a matter of fact—but now he's coming back to marry me. I am sorry, Mr Bacon: I see that I have behaved very badly in not telling you, but I thought you just wanted to be friends."

He shrugged his shoulders, speechless.

"I do realise this must be a bit upsetting—I do really, for certainly I should have let you into my confidence. I want you to know that I'm very fond of you indeed—as a friend; and I sincerely hope we shall not lose touch. Of course, we shall invite you to the wedding; but in case you feel you can't accept, I hope you'll be able to come round for dinner as soon as we get back from our honeymoon."

"I don't think I can, thanks just the same," he replied gruffly, avoiding her eyes. "I expect I shall be leaving for abroad very soon. Point of fact, I'd decided that if you turned me down I'd go out to Canada by myself. There's nowt for me here."

"I think you're very sensible. I'm sure I wish you all the very best of luck," she said, "and I'm sure that Bradshaw would want to be included in that wish. Now, if you'll excuse me, I think I'll take my leave. Perhaps it would be better if I went back to town by train—I have plenty of time. Let's part here, Mr Bacon, but let's part good friends."

She extended her hand. He shook it automatically, looking down at his feet.

"Look at me, Herbert," she said gently: "Adieu, my friend, and God bless you."

He turned on his heel, and groped his way to the car. The door slammed, the starter whirred, the gears ground, and he was off. She watched him disappear down the lane they had just walked; then, with a sigh of relief mingled with resignation, she walked towards the bus stop to find out how soon she could get back to Worthing. Perhaps she should splash and take a taxi. She ought to be getting back to Ebury Street as soon as possible—poor old Bradshaw would be worrying himself to death.

Chapter Eight

I

It was nearly eight o'clock when Margaret got back to Ebury Street. She closed the front door behind her, grateful for its solidity, and stood for a minute in the dark, musty hall, for once enjoying the familiarity of the smell of leaking gas and the day's cooking. After all, whether she liked it or not, this was the smell of home, or at least the threshold of it; and there was her dear, faithful bicycle propped up against the, wall, covered with an old sheet to protect it from dust. It rebuked her mutely for her recent neglect, as if it was complaining that the dust-sheet felt more like a shroud, and that it was not yet ready to be discarded.

"I am not going to put up with Mrs Twitcher's constant complaining any more," she thought, feeling a sudden spasm of indignation. Dangling her white handbag from her elbow, she grasped the machine by the frame and handlebars, and carried her dear old cycle up to her own, dear little room. She hoped that the dust-sheet would protect her poppy-silk dress—not that it mattered very much if it didn't.

She had left the windows closed in case of a storm, and the place was like an oven. She rested the bike against the wardrobe wall—by no means a bad place to keep it permaently. She opened the two sashes, and pulled down the blinds. With a sigh of relief, she stepped out of her sandals, unpinned her hat, and slipped out of her dress. She undressed completely, rolling up all her underclothes and stuffing them straight into the laundry-bag that hung inside the dark wardrobe. Everything she had worn for today's exertions would have to be washed.

She luxuriated in her freedom from sticky clothes, stretching her arms high above her head, and feeling the caress of the faint, Ebury Street breeze. She noticed in the wardrobe mirror that she was still wearing her white gloves, and she had to laugh at herself, standing there all naked except for them. Well, it wasn't such a bad idea to keep them on while she did the housework, for they would have to be washed, too.

She took from the chest o' drawers a large white apron, slipped it over her head, and tied it behind her. With a new yellow cloth, she dusted thoroughly every surface in the room, swept the grey carpet, and wet-mopped every inch of the linoleum with a bucket of hot water laced with disinfectant. She emptied the bucket down the sink, then scoured the sink with more disinfectant. She stripped off the soiled white gloves, scrubbed her hands as if she was about to unbandage a septic wound, and remade her bed with an entire set of clean linen.

She took off the apron, slipped on her blue flannel dressing-gown, and with her sponge-bag dangling from her hand and a clean white towel over her arm, set out for the bathroom on the landing. She put sixpence into the old brass geyser, and with the first hot water, scoured the bath; then she filled the bath and scoured herself with her loofah till she was pink and tingling all over.

Back in her room, she shampooed her hair, rinsing it with an eggcupful of vinegar to get the soap out; she trimmed her nails, fingers and toes, collecting all the slivers with the utmost care in an old envelope to throw in the waste basket.

She was very hungry, but she couldn't decide quite what she fancied. In the end, she scrambled herself two eggs, but the first forkful so turned her stomach that she couldn't touch them, and had to throw them straight into the garbage bin under the sink. She ate a slice of brown bread and drank three cups of tea, and that was sufficient.

When the dishes were put away, she took down from the top of the wardrobe one of the blankets she had discarded for the summer, a soft, fluffy Witney, practically new. She took off her dressing-gown and climbed into bed, hugging the blankets and loving the coolness of the sheets, the tickly hairiness of the soft blanket against her flesh. It smelt slightly of camphor—such a *clean* smell!

"Bradshaw," she whispered, "I've had such a ghastly day it just isn't true. I suppose I've behaved badly to that man, but what on earth could I do? I mean he was simply beastly! Quite frankly, dear-heart, I just can't stand anybody messing me about, and to have to go to bed with anyone but you—ugh! It's utterly unthinkable..."

With a sigh of content, the warm presence in her arms giving her a delicious sense of security, she slipped into the sweet oblivion that deep-down she felt she had earned.

II

For the first weeks her affair with Bradshaw progressed well, with lapses that seemed no more than occasional. Herbert Bacon was not in the office on Monday morning, and did not appear again; he had vanished like a bad dream. Rumours about him kept the typists' room happy for a score of tea-breaks—Mr Bacon was ill; he had been in a car crash; he had embezzled the petty cash and had gone behind the Iron Curtain; he had eloped with Mr Boothby's only daughter, Petronella, who was an artist in Paris, and he was living with her in sin. Margaret Finlay refused to listen to such stuff: she had more important things on her mind.

First and foremost she had to eat more to keep up her strength. She took to having rather larger breakfasts than had been her wont—porridge, two eggs, toast, butter and marmalade, and at least three cups of tea. At eleven o'clock she nipped out of the office to go to Lyons' for a bath-bun and a cup or two of milky coffee. When pressure of work kept her at her typewriter, she nibbled somewhat furtively milk chocolate with nuts and raisins—after all, she could hardly afford to feed the whole typists' room! At lunch-time she went to a disreputable-looking café where they fried great pans full of sausages, onions, and chips. Here she could eat as much as she needed without embarrassment for her unladylike appetite, for no one she knew ever came in, and no one there took any notice of her. At four, she had a cup of tea in the office, then darted over to Lyons' again for a doughnut, or a piece of sponge-cake. Back at Ebury Street, in the evenings, she served soup, a nourishing meat course, and to follow fresh fruit and biscuits, or stewed prunes and rice. Last thing at night, before retiring, she drank a glass of milk.

She ate nourishing foods, but often she had to force them down because of insufficient appetite. She put on a good deal of weight, so that she burst all her seams and had to buy a new skirt. Funnily enough, her face remained very much the same: she peered at herself in the long mirror before her bath, and had to chuckle at her little face on the swelling body.

"Good Heavens, Bradshaw," she once commented, "look what you're doing to me! I'm growing as large as a cart-horse!"

She had her bad moments, of course, and when these occurred she got very angry with herself. She told herself that she was an ungrateful wretch, with not the slightest cause to complain at her lot. She had a loving companion who fitted in with her personality completely, who shared the same bed and the same room without the slightest discord. Doubtless, she was one of the luckiest women in England; and if, because of so complete a *rapport*, there was a certain emptiness in their relationship at times, perhaps through the very lack of any real diffevences of opinion, it was surely a small price to pay for such harmonious companionship.

III

It was in the evenings after dinner that she felt most discontented. She would wash up the dishes, then sit down opposite Bradshaw on the bed to pour out coffee.

"Well, dear-heart," she would say, "what do you feel like doing this evening? Shall we go to a film, or shall we stay at home and paint?"

But Bradshaw seemed unresponsive and lifeless, and more evenings than not, she would go out for a walk by herself. Because these walks were always lonely, they were also rather sad. It was September, and though the weather was still beautiful, there was a slightly melancholy deepening of colours, as if the very leaves were tired of the sun, and waiting for the autumn winds to shake them from the branches to merciful death.

One Sunday afternoon she was walking through Hyde Park, wishing Gran were with her, and thinking how you never really got over the death of someone you loved, when she saw a couple lying side by side on the grass without touching. Something about them fascinated her: she found a seat so that she could watch them whilst pretending to look at the boats on the Serpentine.

They inched towards each other, as if they were being drawn to their mutual destruction like air bubbles on a cup of tea. In fascination and horror she watched the two bodies become one; and then the male glued his mouth to the female's, forcing her down under his weight, she felt that she must scream or faint with disgust. Trembling and giddy, she rose from her chair, and forced herself to walk away.

To soothe herself she walked whither she knew not, and to her astonishment found herself by the river near Hammersmith Bridge. What on earth was she doing out here? She had walked miles without knowing it, and was now faint with fatigue and thirst. She ran up to two policemen who were walking in their authoritative, unhurried way.

"Excuse me," she said a little out of breath, for she had some weight to carry these days, "can you tell me how to find a public-house called The Dove?"

Why on earth she wanted The Doves when any pub near to hand would have done equally well, she couldn't fathom; but she listened to the policemens' directions carefully, and after some fifteen minutes and two blind alleys, found the place she had asked for.

She walked into the public bar, but the noise of the crowd so much terrified her that she walked straight out again. "Margaret, this is sheer cowardice," she muttered, and forced herself to go back in once more, to push her way to the counter, and to ask loudly and forcefully for a shandy.

"Lemonade or ginger-beer?" the barman asked.

"Ginger-beer."

"Pint or half-pint?"

"Pint."

She grasped the foaming tankard by the handle, and took it into the farthest, darkest corner of the room where no one would notice her. She gulped down so much so fast that she spluttered, and some came down her nose. She forced herself to put the drink quietly on the glass-topped table before groping in her handbag for her hanky. After she had repaired the damage, she looked stealthily round the room. It was crowded with fat, red-faced men with pig eyes, and nasty, common women wearing too much makeup, whose eyes were of stone. They were all horrid, and there was no one there she either knew, or wanted to know, so she took her drink and went out on to the veranda. That, too, was crowded, and where once she and Herbert had sat, there was a perfectly horrid woman in brown slacks, lean and tough as a greyhound, with a great fat walrus of a man with a moon face and a houndstooth jacket; and in all the crowd was not a single friendly face. They were all enemies. Why had she ever come to this place? She had no idea, but she wanted to leave at once, without waiting to finish her drink—it was bitter and sick-making in any case. Her aching feet carried her away from the hubbub and smoke and stink of beer to the bus stop, and a nice, friendly, nearly empty bus carried her back to Victoria.

Only when the door of her room was locked behind her could she breathe again.

"Bradshaw," she said, "how wise you were to stay quietly at home! I've walked myself off my feet, and I didn't enjoy my afternoon one bit. Point of fact, it was simply frightful! I shall not do this sort of thing ever again—I don't know what came over me, I'm sure! What I need now is a good hot bath, and afterwards some cold milk and a couple of chocolate biscuits, perhaps. After that, dear-heart, I don't know about you, but I shall be quite ready for beddiebyes."

Bradshaw agreed wholeheartedly.

IV

But the week-end following, Bradshaw was again poor company. He was entirely charming—*gentil comme tout*, as the French say—in the very early morning and last thing at night, but during the day his inanity got on her nerves.

That Saturday, after putting up with his airiness for two hours, she told him to get out of the house and leave her to clean up the place in peace.

"Go into the country for the day," she told him, "and for goodness' sake get some exercise and some fresh air—you haven't stirred from this room for weeks. Don't come back till midnight! By then I may have a surprise for you."

As soon as he had gone, she ran to the Army and Navy Stores, where she bought gallons of white, rubber-base paint and a lambskin roller. She put on her oldest clothes and a pair of gym shoes, and covered all the furniture with newspaper. She painted so fast that by four o'clock she had finished all four walls and the ceiling. She soaked in a long, hot bath, then took herself for a special treat to the Roxy for a special programme of three Westerns she had had her eye on all week.

She enjoyed herself enormously! There were lots of galloping horses, and lots of cowboys shooting at each other, punching each other flat, and waiting in ambush to kill each other. She loved every minute!

When Bradshaw returned at midnight, she was already in bed in a gleaming white room, sipping warm milk and honey.

"Good Lord!" Bradshaw said in his dry way, "it looks like a blooming hospital, but point of fact it looks very fresh and clean, lass."

"I thought you'd like it, dear-heart," Margaret replied, "you're as much a stickler for cleanliness as me. Now go and have your bath like a good boy, and come to bed. I'm dog-tired."

V

The following Saturday Margaret decided that this time she would take a day off, and leave Bradshaw at home. Under the September sun, cooler now but none the less beautiful, she cycled northwards into Hertford, having a mind to go to Hatfield to see the palace where the Virgin Queen, Elizabeth I, spent her childhood. The *Blue Guide* said that the gardens were particularly lovely.

She left the Great North Road as soon as possible, and meandered down a winding lane that rose and fell over gentle hills in a pleasingly energetic way. At about three in the afternoon she came to a charming village of warm red brick, grey stone, and white plaster under thatched roofs. The church was small but sturdy—Norman, of course.

Inside it was austere, with simple oaken pews, but for a rather ugly, brass lectern, curlicue and Victorian. To the right of the organ was a small chapel whose walls were bare and white—like her own, dear little room! There was a big square sarcophagus of white marble in the centre, on which reclined a crusader and his wife, side by side. His hands were clasped in prayer over the hilt of a mighty sword, hers over a prayer book, and their dog lay at their feet. Round the casket on which they rested were their descendants, their faces worn and indistinct. The crusader's face was rough but strong, with curling moustaches and a pointed beard; his wife's was austere but serene, as unworldly as a nun's.

Margaret cried out in delight and ran to get her sketching block from her saddle-bag, to get as much work in before the light failed. She sketched furiously till dusk filled the church and she could see no more. She folded her block with a sigh and straightened her back, for squatting on the stone floor had given her a crick in the back, and her sit-upon was numbed and half frozen. It was suddenly chilly in the little chapel, and her arms went goose-fleshy. It was still and shadowy; a great distance away a door banged shut. It was as if she were the crusader's wife, and interred in the cold tomb for ever . . .

Hurriedly, Margaret left the church, and stuffing the sketching-block into her saddle-bag, pedalled away from death into the life of the village. She found a snug little tea-shop where she warmed her blood with two soft-boiled eggs, brown bread and butter, home-made plum jam, several home-made cakes, and at least four cups of strong tea. She thought how comforting such simple refreshment was! The world outside was dark and chilly, full of ghosts and loneliness, and in that small shop was light and warmth and encouragement, a sign that life could be good, in spite of the dreariness of death that inevitably waited in the shadows.

She paid the bill and strode out into the night, a warrior full of fight. She clicked on her dynamo-lamp, mounted, and spurred her faithful steed towards Ebury Street.

VI

She went to a film on the way home, and didn't get in till nearly eleven. Her room was cold. She lit the gas-fire and went for a hot bath, but when she returned the cold was still there.

"Perhaps it's me," she thought, and putting on the kettle for a hot-water bottle, made herself a mug of nice hot milk sweetened with honey. She snuggled up in the armchair very close to the fire, and looked at the sketch she had done—the crusader's wife utterly cold, utterly still, on her tomb. It was a good drawing—

too good, in fact: she shuddered slightly, and covered it up, for it made her feel funny.

She finished her milk, filled the hot-water bottle, jumped quickly into bed, and turned out the light. Under the bedclothes, she snuggled up to Bradshaw.

"Dear-heart, I'm cold," she whispered. "Warm me! I feel as if I'm made of stone."

Bradshaw's warmth, his soft hairiness against her, turned her from cold marble to flesh and blood. Margaret Finlay was alive again—Princess M., the daughter of a soldier and a soldier herself, advancing into battle on her splendid charger, gold armour flashing in the sun. Behind her was the battle-line of knights, all dependent on Princess M.'s courage and beauty for their success in battle, for she was their inspiration. She unfurled her father's banner, a blood-red lion on a white background, and held up aloft on her glittering lance.

"Advance," she cried, and spurred her gallant steed to a canter. She could hear the drumming hoof-beats of the war-like knights at her back; she saw the lines of the enemy drawn up before her, the sunlight on their armour, the richly-coloured plumes waving in the breeze. Her charger was galloping now full tilt, his hoofs pounding the turf. The Royal banner flapped in the breeze, her golden hair streamed out behind her, the great horse rose and fell under her.

"Charge," she cried, "charge . . ."

The flying horse suddenly shuddered and crumpled to his knees, an enemy arrow quivering in his throat. A great stream of blood gushed forth from it—life blood! The blood of her most gallant companion-of-the-bosom, Bradshaw! The enemy had killed him.

She was no longer M., the beautiful, fighting princess. She was the crusader's wife, waiting for the return of her lord from the

Holy Land, anguish and despair mounting in her heart. She had spent her days bravely, ordering the affairs of the great castle with the utmost efficiency; superintending the embroidery of the great tapestry, the chronicle of the times. When fear and uncertainty engulfed her, she retreated to her private chapel to pray. But her lord was never to return through the iron gates through which he had so bravely set forth. Instead there came a weeping messenger, his arms-bearer, to tell her of a soldier's death without the sun-baked walls of some alien city, and of the Turkish arrow that had pierced a gallant throat.

White to the lips, the blood pounding in her temples, she rose in silence, and with a nod to her weeping women to leave her undisturbed, walked to the chapel where she could lament his death in solitude; for a soldier's wife must bear pain with dignity, even the pain of a loss that condemned her to loneliness perpetual until the merciful release of death.

"But at least she had a real man," Margaret Finlay gasped out loud, "—Oh, God, I can't stand it any more!" Her despair was as sharp as a knife. With loathing, she threw from her bed to the floor the rumpled white blanket she had clutched to her. Now she knew what she had felt ever since childhood, that there could be no comfort for her except death, for she was under the curse of sterility. She knew her fate:

> To them that hath shall much be given, but to them that have not, even that which they have shall be taken away.

She had had a friend, a good friend, and she had lost him for the sake of a dream. Now, she had lost the dream also, and must live in a cold tomb for the rest of her days till the great darkness engulfed her.

VII

She slept deeply and woke late on Sunday morning, much refreshed. The sun was pouring in through the two-sash windows, filling the white room with warm light. Lying in bed, her head cradled in her arms, she thought over her last night's depression. Partly, of course, it was sheer fatigue; but it was not to be dismissed only at that! Loneliness and death were very real—as real as decay of the body and old age.

"I must accept it," she told herself fiercely; "I must accept it.'" She had been lonely all her life, so it was nothing new. Only, she had allowed a childhood game to become too complete an escape from the bitter truth: that was her fault. She had put too much burden on Bradshaw, and Bradshaw had sunk to his knees under it. If she treated Bradshaw rightly, he could still be the most entertaining of companions. If she tried to rely on him for everything, he would certainly fail her, and she would finish up in the insane asylum.

She rose, dusted the room, made the bed, and cooked herself some breakfast. Afterwards, she had a great desire to write a letter, but to whom? Daddy hadn't yet replied to the one she had written at Easter, in which she had begged him to write back promptly. Besides, he owed her a dozen letters at least, and it seemed pointless to keep on posting letters which were never answered. Who else was there? No one, point of fact. There was only M.'s journal.

She took it from the drawer, unscrewed her pen, and began to write:

Sunday, September 12th.
Life is very hard, lonely and miserable. I am very frightened of death, and I don't want to grow any older. I am certain this is true of a lot of people, but most of them never think about it.

They play games like falling in love or making lots of money or being successful actors so that they will never have to recognise the truth.

I am sure it is dangerous not to recognise the truth, and even if it isn't dangerous it is cowardly. It is for this reason alone that I despise those ridiculous and superficial women I work with, for they never stop pretending to each other and to themselves. I want none of their nonsense.

But there isn't any harm in passing away the time on a dreary journey in telling stories, and if there isn't anyone to whom to tell stories, why not pretend there is? This is what Bradshaw and I may do. What I may not do is believe he is as real as people. There really isn't Bradshaw. He's just a game. Herbert Bacon was not a game; he was real.

On an impulse, she glanced back at the pages preceding the one she was writing on, and the memory of the summer overcame her till her throat ached. What was he doing now, Herbert Bacon? Had he gone to Canada yet as he had planned? It would be nice to see him again, but probably he wouldn't want to see her after the way she had behaved. Of course, it was only partly her fault, and she shuddered when she thought of what he had tried to do that day; but she would have liked to shake him by the hand again, and wish him good luck, if nothing else. If only she had his address she would write to him. Well, it was no good crying over spilt milk. She had best stop moping and go out for a brisk walk in the park.

"Come on, Bradshaw, let's get some fresh air," she said.

VIII

Without meaning to, she walked to the church on Campden Hill where Gran was buried, which she hadn't visited since she had come up to London from school at the end of her first term, in order to attend Gran's funeral.

The tombstone was of polished granite, and stood at the foot of a gnarled oak. The inscription was simple:

> Here lies Millicent Sarah, wife of Colonel Robert Gordon Finlay, who died serving his country at the battle of Gallipoli. Evermore mourned by those who loved her, R. I. P.

> "My soul doth magnify the Lord, and my spirit hath rejoiced in God my Saviour.
> "For He hath regarded the lowliness of His handmaiden."

The grave looked bleak and uncared-for, a few tufts of grass springing from the sullen, London soil.

"Poor Gran! Poor, poor Gran!" Who really gave a button for the mouldering bones that lay under that granite lid? Under most of the other gravestones there were a few cut flowers, even if they were wilting, and even if they were in chipped vases. On Gran's last restingplace, there was not so much as a jam-jar! "Evermore mourned," indeed! What a lot of hypocritical rubbish! Did her son ever give his mother a thought, any more than he gave his daughter?

"Dear-heart," Margaret muttered, "from now on I'll come every Sunday and bring some flowers—you always loved flowers so much! And every Sunday, I'll spend a little while here chattering to you about the old days, when we went to the park together and told stories."

Even if there was nothing of Gran but dust, it would be a decent and comforting thing to recall her memory.

Chapter Nine

I

The first Monday in October began as a mild, sunny day, which Margaret rather enjoyed as she cycled to the office. It was a calm morning, and she got through her work easily, managing a fifteen minutes' coffee break at about eleven, and a protracted visit to the ladies' at about twelve.

She sat in the narrow, high-ceilinged cubicle, delighting in her privacy, and she thought that these moments of retreat from the senseless noise and chatter of people were amongst the most enjoyable of her life. She had always found a measure of peace in these comfortable tombs, and had always been able to furnish each of them to her satisfaction. At Aylestone it had been the cabbage-green bathroom, the bath on claw legs, its inside scarred black under the tarnished brass taps which had never ceased to drip; the seat had been mahogany, and to flush the bowl you had to pull a sort of hand-brake, which made Margaret into either an engine-driver or a ship's engineer, bound for either London or India the destination depending on her and Bradshaw's mood.

At school the walls had been white, with a pine seat and a pine door to match, and the cistern hung from the wall above. It was stamped "New Era," an exciting name, full of possibility! From it great serpentine pipes ran to the floor and disappeared. That had been Princess M.'s fortified tower, from which she could pour moulten lead on the heads of her enemies if it became necessary.

The toilet in the hostel had really been the prettiest of them all, with its snow-white tiles and sky-blue ceiling. That bowl was called "Twyford's Civic," which was an institution sort of name; but it was all very modern, with a white earthenware cistern behind the back that was operated by a chrome lever like a car door. That had been Margaret Finlay's elegant penthouse flat in Chelsea, with every possible luxury, and a superb view over the river.

At dear old Ebury Street, the toilet was a dark little room next to the bathroom where she spent as little time as possible. After all, she had no need to seek privacy there when she had her own lovely bed-sitter, which she had never tried to imagine as anything other than it was. But at the office, she really needed a little place of her own where every now and then she could escape the interminable chatter of typists and typewriters. This room, with its lofty tiled wall, its ochre ceiling, its mahogany door and partition, had been a number of things, from a private chapel to the dressing-room of an enormously successful and beautiful actress, whose genius was a household word . . . "Did you see Margaret Finlay's *Juliet*?" everyone was asking. "My dear, an absolute triumph!"

She died that night so powerfully that the audience literally sobbed! When it came to the curtain calls, they cheered and clapped and stamped, refusing to let her go; finally they all stood up; "*Bravissimma! Bravissimma!*" they shouted, and kept on shouting till she'd waved them to attentive silence.

"I only want to say," she said, her voice thrillingly beautiful, "that it is I who have to thank you for being a wonderful, wonderful audience! Pony Bradshaw and I both feel that we were only able to give of our best in this wonderful play because of your wonderful attention and sympathy. We want to say, both of us—

God bless you all!" The applause was thunderous, and down the aisle came two—no, three ushers, their arms loaded with great bouquets of flowers—lilies, white as snow, and roses red as blood, and fluffy pink carnations in a huge, horseshoe wreath.

She retreated from the noise of acclamation to the stillness of her dressing-room. She sat now at her mirror—a miniature lake circled with a promenade of brilliant lights—utterly exhausted with her efforts, her beautiful artist's hand covering her face . . .

The outside door clicked and hissed. Immediately she was on her guard.

"What d'you think of that, Glad? Old Eggs-and-bacon coming in just to say good-bye to us all. Nice of him, wasn't it?" Norma Gracewell's voice! Margaret felt all the blood drain from her head. She listened like a deer straining for the baying of the hounds.

"Yes, it was nice of him," Gladys Peach answered. "Lend me some of your Kleenex, Norm, there's a dear."

"Here you are, ducks, coming over. Well, I've got an idea our Herbert didn't come just to say 'bye 'bye to everyone. I think he was looking for Miss Finlay. Here, lend us your tangerine lipstick, there's a sport."

"Oh, all right, but don't waste it: Max Factor isn't cheap, you know! You're silly, Norma—Mr Bacon never had anything to do with Margaret Finlay."

"That's where you're wrong, Miss Know-all. He was as sweet as pie on her in the summer! I know 'cos once I saw them having lunch together in the garden by the church."

"You're out of your mind, how could any man want anything to do with that great rabbit! There's nothing to her except a stomach; all she ever cares about is food! Have you seen how fat she's getting? I've never seen anyone put on so much weight. I'm not surprised, though, the way she gobbles sweets and chocolates all day long, and never offers them to a soul. If you don't mind, I'll have my lipstick back, Norma Gracewell—you've already smeared it on an inch thick! Come on, if you want to have lunch with me at Lyons' you'd better hurry up."

"Ow, all right, I'm just coming. 'Ere's your lipstick back, old meanie, I don't like it anyway—it looks like furniture polish to me—but thanks just the same. I still think you're wrong about Eggs-and-bacon, the first place he looked was her chair, and he didn't 'arf look blue when she wasn't there."

"Oh, rubbish, Norma. Do come on!"

"I'm just coming! It isn't 'arf exciting, our 'erbert sailing for Canada tomorrow. I wish I was going, too! Ow, well, only got another three months in this old dump before Johnny and I sail for the States..."

The door hissed and clicked shut, and their voices receded.

II

Margaret Finlay arranged her skirt, rinsed her hands under the tap, and raced up the stairs to the office without waiting for the lift. It was empty except for the office manager, Mr Bushie, who sat at his desk checking contracts.

"Mr Bushie," she panted, "did Mr Bacon come here while I was away?"

"Why yes, Miss Finlay, you've just missed him. He came in to say good-bye to everyone, and left about five minutes ago. He's sailing to Canada tomorrow, I believe."

"Did he leave any address?"

"Yes, as a matter of fact he did. Care of the Cunard Line, Montreal. All his mail is to be forwarded there."

"But don't you know his London address?"

"I know his old address. It's here: eight Fairfax Terrace, Putney. The phone number is Putney nine, double three, seven."

"Thank you very much, Mr Bushie, I'll just take that down. I want to wish him good luck before he sails."

III

He might possibly have gone to search for her in their old rendezvous. She ran out into the street coatless, which was a bit silly, but she didn't want to miss a chance of catching him.

She raced along to the Tower Gardens, and walked slowly along by the river scanning the benches. There were fewer people than in the summer, but no Herbert. The same children played soldiers with the old black cannon, making the same noises of battle. It was colder now than it had been in the morning, and there was the smell of fog in the air. The sun was large and red, but there was no warmth in it.

Might he have gone to that public house he had taken her to for their first lunch? She broke into a run, galloped through the gates of the Tower, past the khaki-uniformed sentry who must have thought her crazy, and raced across the cobbles.

She arrived very much out of breath, and climbed straight up the stairs to the dining-room, the blood pounding in her ears. The same buzz of conversation, the same smell of food, beer, and tobacco, no Herbert. Her heart sank.

"There's a table in the corner, Miss."

"It's all right, thank you, I was just looking for someone."

Slowly, very little hope left, she walked to the garden of All Hallowes—"Please, God, let him be there," she prayed. There were two dirty old men in torn macintoshes, peering at folded newspapers; there was a sparrow or two hopping down the sandy path, searching unsuccessfully for crumbs.

It was no good, he was gone, just as Bradshaw had gone when she went off to school. It was no good pretending that Herbert was hiding in the darkest corner of her mind, waiting to appear when Miss Pritchard had gone to the village, or the Headmistress had stopped jabbering: Herbert was real, not a dream; and he had gone to Canada to make his fortune. She might just as well resign herself to the fact, and go and have a good, hot lunch to cheer herself up. Meat pudding and chips, perhaps.

IV

Then she saw him. He was in that old navy raincoat of his, just disappearing into Tower Hill Underground. Her heart jumped and pounded, her knees went as soft as pillows, and in a nightmare she tried to cross to him before he went down the stairs; but she couldn't—the traffic wouldn't let her! Desperate, she made a dash for it; there was a screech of brakes, an infuriated hooting, a taxi driver shouting to her that she was a fool, and she reached the pavement.

She galloped through the ticket office and down the stairs.

"Ticket, please," the collector asked. He had a nasty toothbrush moustache, and bloodshot little eyes like a pig with a chill.

"Oh, I haven't got a ticket, but I've just seen a friend who's sailing to Canada tomorrow. I'll buy a ticket at the other end, I promise I will."

"Where will you be alighting, Miss?"

"I don't know. You see I just want to catch my friend before he goes—oh, please let me through."

"Well, all right this time, Miss, but don't go and make an 'abit of it."

She was through, and on the bridge that led to either the east or the west-bound train. Which would he take? The west-bound to Putney? She heard the thunder of the train arriving, muttered a prayer, and made a dash for it.

She was right! She saw the navy raincoat disappear into a coach up the train. She just had time to get through the nearest doors before they slid shut.

The train pulled out. The next stop was Bank: she would have time to change coaches, plenty of time! But now she was so near seeing him again, she wished she wasn't: what on earth would she say? "I just wanted to say, good luck, Herbert . . ." But that was hardly adequate after her rejection of him on Chanctonbury. "Herbert, I want to tell you that I lied to you about Bradshaw. He was just a story, and I only brought him up because I was frightened. Please forgive me. You're really everything that Bradshaw has ever meant, and a good deal more. Don't run away without me." She *couldn't* say that, she just couldn't. It was being such a traitor for one thing, and she didn't even mean it for another. She only wanted to apologise to him for hurting his feelings.

The train began braking for the stop. She waited near the doors, her muscles flexed: as soon as they opened she was away down the platform, galloping like a racehorse for all she was worth. She jumped into the second coach along, but she couldn't see him—could she have made a mistake? She walked to the doors between the compartments. There he was, standing in the next doorway, his back to her, reading a newspaper.

The train jerked into motion, but there was still time to step through the communicating doors from coach to coach—she had seen the guards do it sometimes. She wrenched at the green handle, and the door swung open.

"Careful, lady, you'll get hurt!"

Silly old sheep, warning her of what she knew already. What did he think she was, that old man, a child? Interfering fool! She wrenched at the handle of the second door, had a minute's panic stepping across the swaying gap, then she was through.

"Herbert! Herbert, I'm so glad I've found you..."

It wasn't Herbert. It was a man with a round red face and rimless spectacles.

"I beg your pardon, I've made a mistake."

The blood rushed hotly into her face. She moved down the coach, tripped over someone's shoe, almost collapsed into the lap of an old lady with a large box labelled Bourne and Hollingsworth, and recovered by clutching at the khaki-clad knee of a smirking young soldier. Mumbling apologies, she grasped the strong, wonderfully impersonal handrail by the doors.

She was suddenly furious with herself—she was such a fool! After all, she could telephone him at Putney to wish him luck. She didn't have to hunt him all over London, making an absolute laughing-stock of herself. She made herself thoroughly sick!

Now she could return to the office and as a penance sit through the entire afternoon with no lunch: it was ten minutes to two, and there was no time to eat in any case. It served her jolly well right.

V

The afternoon was sheer misery. Each letter was a trial, and she kept on making errors and having to erase them. She was so slow, in fact, that at four o'clock she was way behind, and unable to go out of the office for anything to eat. She had to make do with what was left of a bag of toffees and two cups of Gladys' horrid tea.

All the time her fingers were tapping out letters and contracts, she was going through conversations with Herbert.

"Oh, it's you!" "Yes, Herbert, I've just phoned to wish you *bon voyage*, bags of good luck, and God bless you. I want to tell you that I'm sorry I hurt your feelings." "That's very good and honest of you, lass." "Oh, no, it isn't at all. I'm not honest and I never have been. I don't have a fiancé, and I've never had any lovers other than . . ." "Bradshaw?" "Yes, Bradshaw, but you need not worry or be jealous of Bradshaw anymore." "Margaret, I don't understand!" "Bradshaw is part of me, and part of my childhood. Bradshaw has been a beautiful dream, Herbert, and beautiful dreams are less important than life. But to know life, you have to be awake; and you, Herbert, dear-heart, you have awakened me with a kiss, like the prince who woke Sleeping Beauty. If you want me, Herbert Bacon, prince amongst men, I am yours." "I . . . I don't know what to say, lass. You've overwhelmed me, that's what. Are you certain that you want to be my wife? To wash and scrub for me, to cook for me, to sew buttons on my shirts, to climb with me to the highest hills, to cross the widest valleys, and to journey wherever I journey, till death do us part?" "Yes, Herbert, I am certain. But are *you* certain?" "Oh, Margaret, lass, need you ask?"

"Herbert Bacon, will you have this woman, Margaret Finlay, to thy wedded wife?" "Aye, I will." "Margaret Finlay, will you have this man, Herbert Bacon, to thy wedded husband?" "Well, I think so." "Come now, do you think so, or do you know so? You must make up your mind, you know." "Well, I want to make one or two conditions. Firstly, that we sleep in separate rooms. Secondly, that hereafter, Herbert Bacon shall change his name by deed-poll to Ponikwer Bradshaw. You see, I'm not awfully keen on becoming one flesh, Herbert—that's why I ask the first. As for the second, I owe a great debt to someone who must suffer very greatly by our marriage, and this is a payment of that debt. Do you agree?" "Of course I agree, lass. What's important to me is our friendship, not the bedroom, and all that nonsense. As for changing my name, didn't you know that I was christened Herbert Bradshaw Bacon?

You can call me Pony as a nickname with pleasure." "Well then, Herbert, I am nearly all yours." "Then let's celebrate. Jump on my back and I'll give you a ride."

> "Ride a cock horse, to Banbury Cross
> To see a fine lady upon a white horse . . ."

"Ow, look out, Miss Finlay, your tea's going over!"

"Gosh, so it is! Thanks, very much, Norma, I didn't notice."

"I thought you were going to spill the lot in your lap and scald yourself."

Margaret shuddered.

"That would have been just horrid!" she said.

VI

On the stroke of 5.30 Margaret walked rapidly out of the office, pulling on her coat as she went. She wheeled her cycle down the corridor and out into Fenchurch Street. It was very foggy: the traffic crawled nose to tail, headlights smothered in a blanket of smog. She had better telephone Herbert at once, before she began the journey home.

She wheeled the machine down Fenchurch Street to a sweet-shop she patronised, which had a public phone and stayed open till 6.0. She parked her bike in the kerb—she didn't want pedestrians to trip over it. First she had to get change, for she had only half a crown in her pocket.

"Good evening."

"Good evening, Miss. What can I get you?"

"A half-pound block of Rowntree's milk, fruit, and nut, and some coppers in change for the telephone, please."

"Very well, Miss."

As soon as she was handed the chocolate, she tore open the package and broke off a large section. She was starving! She said thank you with her mouth disgracefully full—Miss Pritchard would have had a fit! The chocolate was delicious. Praised be Rowntree's for inventing "Motoring": what would she ever do without it?

She slipped the coppers into the box, dialled, and heard the high-pitched whine of number engaged.

"Blow!" she said under her breath. She munched the rest of the bar of chocolate and tried again: the number was still engaged. Blow, blow, blow! She would have to telephone from home.

She went out into the smog, and was just in time to see her bike, knocked down by a large van, and disappear under its rear tyre. A pain in her heart, she ran to the roadside and picked it up. The back wheel was terribly buckled, the spokes all smashed. The van had disappeared, heedless of the damage it had done.

She dragged the poor thing on to the pavement. The pedestrians jostled her impatiently: "Get that thing out of the way, it'll hurt someone!" a man said roughly. Heartless beast! Hadn't the accident happened because she was avoiding anyone's tripping over it? They were ungrateful swine, all of them! Her eyes filled with tears.

It was her fault: she had asked for it, leaving the bike on the kerb in a pea-souper. She had only herself to thank, really. If she'd not been so greedy for chocolate, if she had not been in such a stupid hurry to telephone, it wouldn't have happened. What on earth should she do?

"Keep your head, Margaret Finlay. Take the bike home in a cab, and tomorrow you can take it to be repaired."

"Taxi!" she shouted, for one was just passing; "Taxi!"

"Where to, Miss?"

"Would you please take my bicycle and me to Ebury Street? I've just had an accident."

"Sorry, Miss, I can't take a bike." He drove off into the fog.

Despair engulfed her: she would have to drag the damned thing all the way to Grose's, Ludgate Circus, and by that time they would probably be closed. She hated herself! Death was too good for her!

"Miss Finlay! But what is the matter?"

"Oh, Mrs Fleisch, my bike got knocked down by a van and the wheel's all twisted."

"But you, you are not hurt—no?"

"No, I was just coming out of the sweet-shop when it happened."

"If you are all right, then it is no worry! The bike can be repaired, no?"

"I expect so, but I can't find a taxi to take it—I'll have to wheel it all the way home..."

"*Quatsch*! This you do not have to do, Miss Finlay. If you cannot find a taxi, you can leave it in the office till tomorrow, no? But we will find you a taxi, I think."

"I never thought of leaving it in the office! Thank you very much, Mrs Fleisch."

"Och, this is nothing. Hey, taxi! You there!"

"Where to, Ma'am?"

"Driver, we have had a little accident with the bicycle. If you would be so kind as to help, we will be extremely grateful..."

"I'm not going to take a cycle, not in this weather!"

"Now, driver, we will make it worth your trouble—here!"

Mrs Fleisch took a coin out of her bag and gave it him.

"All right, lady; but mind it don't scratch my upholst'ry—I shouldn't take it, mind, it's against the rules..."

"All right, you break the rules, and you get a tip from my friend when you arrive. Here Miss Finlay, we put the bike in quick!"

Together, they manoeuvred the machine into the back.

"So, now you are all set!' cried Mrs Fleisch, triumphantly; and she whispered to Margaret, "Two shillings tip is enough, I have given him half a crown already."

"I must pay you, Mrs Fleisch. I don't know how to thank you..."

"Rubbish, it is nothing; it is a pleasure, Miss Finlay. Don't worry, you can pay me the two and six tomorrow, I can trust you, no? And tomorrow, you come to me for dinner and we have perhaps a long talk together. Well, cheerio! You are all right, I think."

"Cheerio, Mrs Fleisch—and thank you."

"Where to, Miss?"

"Ebury Street, Victoria: I'll show you the house when we get there."

VII

It was nine o'clock. Margaret was groping her way along Fairfax Terrace, Putney. She was wearing her poppy silk dress under a navy winter overcoat, her white hat, her white gloves and shoes. This was not a very suitable get-up for a foggy night, perhaps, but after her bath she had looked for something to put on and there hadn't been anything else. She'd had to leave off the belt of the poppy dress at that, and tie the blue silken tassels from her dressing-gown round her middle. It looked a little funny, the pink and the blue together, but perhaps Herbert wouldn't notice.

It was a horrible journey to have to make on such a night, but Herbert's telephone had given the engaged signal four times, till she had asked for the operator and had found out the number was out of order. She would have sent him a telegram, but that wasn't enough: she wanted to shake him by the hand before he made the long journey to the New World. So she was groping along what she hoped was the right street, a torch in her hand that illuminated the swirling fog more than anything else, but it did give her just enough light to show her the kerb and the house numbers.

Number 8 and journey's end. It had been one of the most difficult voyages of her life, but now by faith and courage she had arrived. Up the tiled path, up the two steps. Behind the front door was the little flower for which she had been searching ever since she'd been a little girl, the flower which would remove the curse from her father's kingdom. Only, she must keep her head!

She groped for the bell, but couldn't find it. She knocked sharply once, twice, three times. After two minutes, she knocked again, louder, and listened at the letter box. There was a shuffling of slippers and an irritable, croaking, "All right, all right, I'm coming..." The door opened a crack, and a nose and chin peaked out.

"Whatcher want?"

"Mr Herbert Bacon?"

"He isn't here any more, he's gone to Canady."

"Oh, dear, I wanted to see him so much. To say goodbye, you see."

"Well, you're too late."

"But I'm not, he doesn't sail till tomorrow!"

"Well, I don't know about that, Miss. He left today, that's all I know."

"Have you any address?"

"Well, I 'ave, but it's downstairs. Do you really want it?"

"Yes, I do."

"'Oo are you?"

"I'm just a friend. A close friend."

"I s'pose you're the young lady wot made 'im go off, and now you're sorry—eh?"

"I don't see that it's any business of yours. Have you got Mr Bacon's address or not?"

"Ow, all right. Wait a moment. Come inside a moment, then I can close the door."

The slippers shuffled off. Intolerable interference! Women like that should be shot at dawn. Would she ever find Herbert? Would this search go on for the rest of her life? Had they descended from the hill-top only to lose each other in a London fog? Perhaps it was her punishment to have lost him for good, this time. She felt sick!—the house smelt of cats and boiled fish.

The slippers shuffled back.

"'Ere's the address—I can't see very well, you'll 'ave to read it yourself. 'Ere, I'll switch on the light."

Herbert's handwriting on a postcard:

>Herbert Bacon, Esq.,
>c/o Cunard Steamship Company,
>Montreal, Canada.

"Thank you," she said. "Thank you very much." She noticed under the dim light that her white gloves were filthy already, as if she had worn them to scrub floors. God, she hated this fog!—hated it with all her heart!

VIII

She was awake, but keeping her eyes closed to pretend that she was still asleep. Inside was the terrible knowledge that she had lost something very important. Don't think about it, just don't think about it. "Bradshaw, where are you?"

"Bradshaw's left. He's sailing to Canada in the morning, and he's lost in the London fog tonight. What's more, you've gone and ruined your bicycle."

"Mrs Fleisch says the bike can be repaired."

Supposing it can, supposing the frame isn't all twisted, that won't bring Herbert back. He's gone for good! You've done it this time!

"Perhaps he'll telephone before he leaves! He did come to the office to say good-bye to me. Norma *said* he came to say good-bye to me. That's what he'll do! He'll telephone just before he goes . . ."

From a great distance she heard the bell ringing in the corridor. She sat up in bed in the dim, foggy dawn. It couldn't be for her! No one knew her number, except Mr Bushie at the office . . . unless he'd told someone. It might be for Mrs Twitcher, or for one of the other people in the house—a death, or a birth, or a lover's return; or somebody ill, perhaps.

She flew downstairs to the hall, and lifted the receiver off its hook. "Hallo," a gruff Yorkshire voice said, "might I speak to Miss Margaret Finlay?" "It's she speaking," she said, and the hall began spinning around. "Margaret, it's me, Herbert. I'm sorry to get you out of bed, but I tried to telephone last night and you were out—I got your number yesterday from the office. I just wanted to say good-bye and good luck . . ." "Oh, Herbert, I went to your place last night to say good-bye and good luck to you, but you had left." "I'm sorry, lass, what a pity. I spent my last night at a hotel. I'm glad I got hold of you before I left. Oh, Margaret, I do wish you were coming with me." "I wish I were, too." "What did you say, Margaret lass?" "I said, I wish I were coming with you, too. I've missed you very much, Herbert. I didn't mean what I said about Bradshaw being my lover! Bradshaw's really you, you know, but I didn't know it." "Well, you great nincompoop, you, why didn't you say? Come to Canada with me, and we'll start that tea-shop together." "But I'm not packed, or anything! I haven't got a ticket even . . ." "Never mind all that, I'll fix all the details! I'll pick you up in two hours time. Pack a suitcase or two with what you need..."

"Miss Finlay," cried Mrs Twitcher, scandalised, "what in 'eaven's name are you doing with no clothes on, on a morning like this?—you'll catch your death, you will, and with nothing on your feet, too."

"I . . . I thought I heard the phone ringing, Mrs Twitcher."

"I didn't hear nothing."

"The phone did ring, but it went off as soon as I got to it. I was expecting a call, you see. What time is it, Mrs Twitcher?"

"'Arf seven, Miss Finlay. 'Adn't you better get some clothes on, Miss Finlay? Some of the gentlemen might be coming down in a minute or two."

"Yes, Mrs Twitcher, I'm just going."

IX

She had to go to the office by Underground, walking like other mortals to the station.

Shadows in the fog on the way; they came within a yard or two, so that she could recognise them as people, then they disappeared, poor ghosts, into the fog.

Inside she was cold and grey, with a great emptiness. What was there to live for now? Food?

The fog was choking her! She wanted to get out of it—she had to get out of it before it killed her! But perhaps it would be better to give up, to let the fog do its work, and change her into feelingless smoke. After all, what was the point in fighting on? She was sick of the whole miserable business of living! It would be so easy, so pleasant, to take some pills and go to sleep, drifting into a grey cloud of nothingness for ever. No one would care, after all.

X

Margaret sat in the typists' room alone. It was one o'clock, just the time that she and Herbert used to meet down in the corridor by her bike, to go out to lunch together. How warmly Herbert used to smile when he saw her, with his eyebrows all shaggy like an airedale. And now he had disappeared, perhaps for ever.

How the yellow grey smog smothered the city! It penetrated everywhere, till even the air in the office was poisoned.

She forced herself to look away from the dirty window to the blank sheet of paper between the rollers. Staring at the smog wouldn't get the letter written, and if she didn't hurry up and get it done, the girls would be back, and she would have sacrificed her lunch-hour in vain.

Dear Herbert (she wrote),

It is difficult to write this letter, so excuse me if it seems a bit confused. First of all, I want to say how sorry I am I missed you yesterday, for I would like to have wished you good luck.

Secondly, I must tell you how deeply sorry I am for my silliness on Chanctonbury. Herbert, I don't know how to tell you this, but it's not true that I am, or ever was, engaged to Bradshaw. There isn't anyone called Bradshaw except in my imagination. In some ways, Herbert, you are much more Bradshaw than ever Bradshaw was.

Whatever you think of me, don't let yourself be hurt by my idiotic behaviour. If you can bring yourself to forgive me, I should dearly love to hear from you, God speed, dear-heart.

Love,
Margaret.

She was typing out the envelope, her eyes smarting, when Gladys Sneath, née Peach, returned.

"Why, it's Miss Finlay," she said, "Have you got back from lunch already?"

"No, Mrs Sneath," said Margaret. "I didn't go to lunch today."

"That's a change for you, isn't it?" said Gladys. "Are you going on a diet or something?"

She hung up her red macintosh, settled herself in her chair, and began filing her sharp, blood-red nails.

"No, I'm not on a diet," said Margaret. "I was writing a letter, if you're interested."

She sealed the envelope and stamped it, gaining a little courage and hope from it as she did so.

"Oh, no offence meant, I'm sure, Miss Finlay," said Gladys.

"And none taken, Mrs Sneath," said Margaret, rising to put on her raincoat to go to the post office.

"Oh, Miss Finlay," honied Gladys, "while we're here alone, may I take the liberty of asking you a personal question?"

Margaret made no pause in her movements.

"If you wish, Mrs Sneath," she said, "but I don't guarantee to answer it."

"Norma tells me she's invited you to her wedding at Christmas."

"That's true," said Margaret.

"But she hasn't invited your fiongcee."

"No," said Margaret, "she hasn't."

"Well, Miss Finlay, George and I want to ask you to dinner, but we don't know whether to ask you and Mr Bradshaw, or not."

"It's very nice of you and George, Mrs Sneath," said Margaret. "When exactly would you want us to come?"

"Well," said Gladys, "we hadn't reely thought of a particular date. When would you both like to come?"

Gladys didn't look too certain of herself.

"How about this Saturday, Mrs Sneath? I could call Bradshaw and ask him if we're free."

"Oh, well I'm afraid George and I can't next Saturday," said Gladys. "We're going to George's parents."

"Very well," said Margaret, "how about Friday?"

"Oh, I'm afraid Friday's no good either."

"Well, how about tomorrow night, or even tonight?"

Gladys blushed.

"I'm afraid that's a bit short notice," she said.

"Then why don't you suggest a date, Mrs Sneath, since you were kind enough to suggest it."

"Well," Gladys faltered, "perhaps it would be better to leave it till after Christmas."

"Why?" asked Margaret.

"Oh, I don't know," cried Gladys peevishly, "because it just might, that's all."

"Very well," said Margaret, "when you're really ready to ask Bradshaw and myself to dinner, please feel free to do so. And if you're just a little curious about my love life, please feel free to pump me whenever you like. You have no need to spend your time speculating, Mrs Sneath. Just ask me and I'll tell you."

Gladys pouted.

"All right, if you want to know I *was* wondering how many of those stories you told us in the summer were true. It all sounded a bit too good, Miss Finlay, but of course you would never tell anyone any lies, would you?"

"If you call your slight exaggerations about yourself and your love life lies," said Margaret, "yes, I tell them, too."

"But at least George isn't just a story," sneered Gladys tightening her lips.

"Meaning that Bradshaw is," said Margaret. "Well, in a sense you're right, of course, just as your George is nothing but a story to me, and probably to you, too. I doubt if anyone other than yourself has any feelings as far as you're concerned, Mrs Sneath, but perhaps I do you an injustice; perhaps you're less self-centred than you appear. I hope so for Mr Sneath's sake."

"Well, I've never been so insulted in my life," said Gladys.

"You surprise me," said Margaret; and she picked up her letter and marched out of the door. She felt better. She even ran down the stairs singing.

> Routs and discomfitures, rushes and rallies,
> Bases attempted, and rescued, and won,
> Strife without anger, and art without malice,
> How will it seem to you, forty years on . . .

"Oh, I'm so sorry, Mrs Fleisch . . ." for she had careered into that lady who was just waiting for the lift at the bottom of the stairs.

"Miss Finlay," said Mrs Fleisch, when she had recovered. "I am delighted to see you for one minute alone. You remember, please, that you are coming with me home for supper tonight. You have not forgotten, no?"

"Oh, no, Mrs Fleisch," Margaret lied, feeling her tummy turn over as she said it. "How nice of you to ask me."

"I didn't want to mention it in front of everyone," said Mrs Fleisch. "Tell me, my dear, you are coming alone, no?"

"Yes, Mrs Fleisch," said Margaret, looking away from those gently inquiring brown eyes under their green lids. "There is only myself, I'm afraid."

"So, that is all arranged," said Mrs Fleisch. We will take the tube together, then. And tell me, will your bicycle be made well again?"

"Oh, Mrs Fleisch, I hope so," said Margaret, the tears starting in spite of herself. "I'm taking it into the shop on Saturday. Thank you so much for helping me last night..."

"But you have already thanked me," said Mrs Fleisch, "and I have done nothing. So, we will have a nice evening together. I am so glad, my dear Miss Finlay. I have been so much looking forward to this for a long time."

"Oh, Mrs Fleisch..." Margaret began, but no words would come. She tried to smile her thanks, then walked rapidly away, blinking.

Chapter Ten

I

Margaret was more than a trifle intoxicated, for Mrs Fleisch—Nola as she insisted Margaret call her—insisted on refilling her glass all through dinner with an innocuous, velvety red wine that had the most peculiar effect on her. She felt so light-hearted she wanted to sing, or giggle, or dance the can-can. Even more peculiarly, though she had never been in the house before, she felt as familiar in it as if she had spent her childhood here.

But how could this be? Nola lived in the top half of a rather shabby and old-fashioned semi-detached house in Kilburn, which was a part of London that Margaret only knew from cycling from Ebury Street to the Great North Road. She thought of Kilburn as a somewhat slummy district, not unlike Victoria, except that the houses tended to be smaller and uglier. Kilburn had a noisy streetmarket that was to be avoided on Saturday mornings if you were in a hurry.

As for Nola's flat, Margaret knew perfectly well that she'd never been inside it in her life. She hadn't even imagined it accurately—the L-shaped settee on which she sat, whose soft, mulberry-coloured velvet clung to her tweed skirt; the heavy circular table, covered with a cloth of fine Brussels lace; the massive desk and bookcase of figured walnut; the sombre oil paintings of flowers and fruit in heavy gilt frames; the bay windows frothy with lace; the worn Persian carpet; the delicate ormolu clock on the white marble mantelpiece—all these things individually were entirely strange to her. Yet, the atmosphere of this room was such that it was almost as if she were coming home. That was why she felt so curiously happy.

Not only the flat, but the inhabitants of it were entirely different to her imaginings. Rudi Wertheim, whom (they told her) had secretly become Nola's husband, was by no means the dark-jewelled, droop-nosed lecher she had once envisaged. On the contrary, he was thin and stooping, with pink cheeks, fair hair, and mild blue eyes behind rimless spectacles. He looked much more like an oculist, or dentist, than a refugee jewellery manufacturer.

He and Nola lived in this flat with Nola's mother, Mrs Katzenstein, apparently because Rudi's first wife had absconded with all Rudi's money. "This is why I have told no one," Nola had cried. "You are the first in the office to know—but you will keep mum, no?" Yes of course she would keep mum. She was honoured to be so trusted.

As for Mrs Katzenstein—which was rather an odd name, be it admitted—she was a tall lady, very thin, with deep blue eyes and a thatch of wild white hair. Her hands were twisted with arthritis, and when she moved it was evidently with much pain; yet her manner was so gracious and her smile so sweet that Margaret got an inexplicable lump in her throat several times during the evening.

How kind these people were! And how positively weird it was that they could make her feel so at home! Perhaps the wine was the only explanation necessary.

"Margaret, why are you smiling?" said Nola, coming in with the coffee. "I don't know, I think it's the wine," said Margaret.

"I think you were having a beautiful fantasy," said Rudi, in his rather high-pitched voice. "She was quiet as a mouse, but she has been wearing such a strange smile..."

"Rudi, leave the girl alone," said Nola.

"But I have said nothing!" Rudi protested. "Only I was asking her about her fantasy. You do not mind, Miss Finlay, no?"

"Not at all," said Margaret. "I was only thinking how different this room is to my idea of it, and yet I feel that I've been here before..."

"Now this is most interesting," said Rudi, leaning forward. "How did you think it would be? Tell me, please."

"Rudi," said Nola, "would you be an angel and help Mother with the dishes?"

"I'm so sorry," said Margaret, "I'd no idea you were washing up. Let me go and help."

"No, my dear," said Nola, "I would like to talk with you a little..."

"But your mother's hands—I mean doesn't it hurt her?"

"No, Margaret," said Nola, "she is having pain all the time whether she moves or not, but it is better for her when she does not always stay in one position. Rudi will help her—they are good friends those two, and talk of art and psychology till Freud himself would scream."

"What it is to be married to a dictator!" Rudi said with a rather nice, boyish smile.

He stood up, very thin and tall, and loped to the door.

"Thank you, honey," said Nola.

"But on one condition," said Rudi. "You will let me have Miss Finlay to myself also. I find her most charming and interesting."

"And he has only been married to me for three months," said Nola, smiling. "You are sorry for me, Margaret, no?"

"Och, Nola!" said Rudi. "She is terrible, Miss Finlay—but I will leave you to your *tête-à-tête*..."

"You take your coffee black?" asked Nola.

189

"Please," said Margaret.

Nola filled two of the fine blue and white Meissen cups and passed Margaret hers.

"Nola, all your china is so lovely!" exclaimed Margaret.

"We have managed to bring some of our things from Germany in 1938," said Nola. "We have had a beautiful house in Berlin, but Mr Hitler commandeered nearly everything—however all this is a long story which I can always tell you. I have more important things to say. Margaret, you think I am your friend?"

"Yes," said Margaret. "You've been so kind to me..."

"No, my dear, I have done nothing. But this is not what I mean. I ask you if you trust me?"

"Yes, I do, very much," cried Margaret.

"Would you excuse me the impertinence if I ask you a question?" asked Nola. "I have wanted to help you so much, and perhaps I can. May I try once."

"Yes, please do," said Margaret, a little apprehensive in spite of the wine. She took a nervous sip of her coffee. It was too hot.

"Margaret, yesterday Herbert Bacon came back to the office to say *au revoir* to us. You have heard of this?"

"Yes," said Margaret. "I heard."

"And he came into the typists' room and you were not there," said Nola.

"No," Margaret whispered. "No, I wasn't."

"I had a funny feeling that he was very sad because of this," said Nola. "Then Gladys and Norma were having an argument after lunch that you and Mr Bacon were good friends. Is this true, Margaret?"

"Yes," said Margaret.

Nola was silent. Margaret looked up at her for a moment—those gentle, probing brown eyes that seemed to see so much.

"My dear," said Nola, "you have no need to tell me anything. I am not like Gladys a scandalmonger—this I think you know. But I am older than you, and if you feel you can trust me, I wish much to help."

"It's so difficult to tell anyone," said Margaret miserably. "I can't tell you what a dreadful thing I did, Nola . . ."

"Please try," Nola persisted.

Margaret fought herself to speak.

"I . . . I'm so afraid you'll think I'm . . ."

"What will I think you?" Nola asked.

"You'll think me—either soft in the head or wicked!"

"Margaret dear, I have been soft in the head, as you say, so many times, and I am so wicked, I think you have no worry. But it is good for you to talk—don't you think?"

"Yes," said Margaret. "I know."

She struggled to find words—to explain about her and Herbert's friendship, and how it had grown till that moment that he had asked her to marry him. No, it wasn't that moment that it had stopped so suddenly—it was when he wanted to do things—no, it wasn't because he had *said* he never meant any harm, and now she knew she believed him. Their friendship had really stopped when she'd told him about Bradshaw—when she'd hurt him more than she could now bear to face.

"Now who is this Bradshaw?" asked Nola softly.

"Bradshaw . . . is a game I played . . . as a child," Margaret faltered. She covered up her face with her hands, pressing her fingers on her eyes till she saw zebra stripes—zebra stripes in squares, in spheres . . .

"Margaret, you must stop this," said Nola, "Margaret, stop this please and look at me!"

Strong fingers took Margaret's wrists and drew them away from her face. For a moment all was night; then through a blur Nola appeared standing in front of her. Nola's face was a smudge, then gradually she came back into focus.

"Margaret, you must never do this again. You promise me?"

"Yes," said Margaret, not knowing what she was promising, but only wanting to reassure Nola.

"So," continued Nola quietly, resuming her seat, "you were frightened of Herbert and you told him you had a fiancé, no?"

"Yes," said Margaret. "Yes, I did."

"Are you sorry now, then."

"Oh, yes," said Margaret. "I'm so dreadfully sorry . . ."

"Why?"

"Because I hurt his feelings," said Margaret.

"Because you hurt him, or because you hurt yourself?" asked Nola.

"Because I hurt him. I didn't hurt myself—did I?"

"Yes, you did hurt yourself," said Nola. "You are in love with Herbert Bacon, no?"

"No," said Margaret, "I can't be in love."

"Why can't you?" asked Nola.

"Because I can't, that's all; I just can't . . ."

"Why not?"

"I'm incapable of it. I'm not a real woman . . ."

"But who says you are not?"

"I know I'm not, I just know," said Margaret. A funny noise gurgled in her throat—she tried to check it and couldn't; she tried to apologise and couldn't; then she was weeping.

"How do you know?"

"Because I can't make love . . . because I just can't. Don't ask me any more, Nola, I beg you. Please don't ask!"

She sobbed, but what for, for heaven's sake? For a girl clambering up a rockery, her skirt tucked into navy bloomers? For the same girl waiting and waiting for Daddy to come and kiss her good night, and waiting in vain? Or was it because the witch-woman was destroying the whole kingdom, and because a great king lay dying for want of a flower which she and Bradshaw alone could find . . .

Gentle, insistent fingers were kneading the taut muscles of her shoulders, smoothly, firmly, massaging them till the convulsive sobs ceased, till the tremulous breathing was soothed, till she lay exhausted, her head buried in her arms.

"Now listen to me," said Nola, still massaging so smoothly and strongly. "You must first try to trust me a little, Margaret; you must believe that I'm fond of you, no?"

Margaret nodded her head without raising it.

"You have not been soft in the head, or wicked in the least," said Nola. "You have been lonely and frightened, and very many people are lonely and frightened even worse than you, my dear. You must learn there is nothing to fear; I will try to help you learn this a little. You will allow this?"

"Yes," Margaret whispered, "yes."

"So," said Nola. "There is one thing you will promise me, please. You will come again to dinner with us on Saturday night. Yes?"

"Yes."

"Now, my dear, I think it would be best if you went home and had a good night's rest. We have talked enough for one evening. Only one thing: I want you to ask yourself this question: since you know that Herbert Bacon loves you, don't you believe that you really love him, also, and that you would like one day to be his wife? Don't tell me anything now. Just think it over to yourself for the next day or two. On Saturday we will talk more of this."

"All right," said Margaret, sighing deeply.

"Now sit up and open your eyes," said Nola. "After all, nothing so terrible has happened—has it?"

The room was full of a bright soft light. It glowed with colour like a Dutch painting. Nola sat down in her chair, and looked at her with those warm brown eyes of hers.

"Would you like Rudi and me to take you home?"

"No," said Margaret, "you've done so much—I feel so grateful . . . I don't know what to say, Nola. Such a thing has never happened to me before . . ."

"You always wish to thank me when it is not necessary," said Nola. "You can understand this, perhaps. When I needed help, someone has also given me very much. So now when I see you need help, I can return a little of what I have had. Then one day, you will help someone else also, you will see. That is how we manage to survive."

She went to the door and opened it.

"Rudi . . . Mutti . . ." she called. "Are you two flirting again?"

Mrs Katzenstein came into the room smiling.

"*Och, Nola, du bist schrecklich*," she said. 'My daughter says to me the most dreadful things," she explained to Margaret, "but all daughters are alike, I think. They do not respect age, unfortunately."

Rudi loped back to his chair.

"So," he said, "now you two women have finished pulling me to shreds . . ."

"Darling," said Nola, "we have not mentioned you—I am so sorry."

"Well, you make me astonished, but there it is. So, now we will listen to some music a little."

"I think Margaret is tired, dear," said Nola. "We will call a taxi and take her home, yes?"

"Yes," said Rudi; "but I will take her with pleasure in the car."

"Isn't it too foggy?" asked Nola. "We will get lost, no?"

"No," said Rudi, striding to the window and drawing aside the curtain. "The fog is lifting. It is much better."

"Good, then we'll go by car."

"But you have no need to come," said Rudi. "Why don't you stay with Mutti in the warm?"

"Come," said Nola with a smile, "you may flirt with Margaret on Saturday when she is also coming..."

"But I can go by tube," said Margaret. "Really, I'd much rather..."

"*Quatsch*," said Nola, "which is German for nonsense. Rudi honey, you will bring us our coats?"

"*Och, Nolalein*, wait a moment," said Mrs Katzenstein. "I will make you a hot drink before you go out into the cold. Some milk and honey, no?"

"Then Miss Finlay can hear a record—just one," said Rudi. "Beethoven's first piano concerto played by Gieseking."

"You are not too tired?" Nola asked Margaret.

"No, no I should love to hear it," said Margaret.

Then as Nola's mother got up to go to the kitchen, Margaret suddenly realised just what had been at the back of her mind all evening. Mrs Katzenstein was awfully like Gran! And, somehow, this house was awfully like Gran's house.

II

Walking to Victoria Underground, Margaret knew what they meant by "the morning after the night before." The fog had cleared from the city to concentrate inside her head, a pea-soup cloud between one part of her poor old brain and the other, while her tongue felt like old carpet. It was no good; she was not one of the drinking breed.

Last night she'd been as happy as a skylark; this morning she felt ghastly. In her heart was the old pain in a new and more acute form—it was all very well admitting to Nola under the influence of too much wine that she loved Herbert, but how true was it now in the grey light of morning? How true was it, descending the escalator into the hellish, scurrying crowd of mean-faced, evil-smelling clerks? That smell of tobacco and stale bodies and disinfectant, wasn't it awfully like his smell?

On the platform, she tried to stand a little apart from the mob, wishing to goodness that her bike would be ready in time to spare her this ordeal tomorrow. To be independent again, to fly to and from her work without being interfered with—that was all she asked of life. All this business about love was so much talk—she didn't need anyone, she only wanted to be left in peace.

She looked up at the station clock, and peered anxiously down the tunnel—if a train didn't come soon she was going to be late. That was the worst part of public transport, it was so unreliable. With her beloved bicycle she always knew exactly how long it would take her to get to the office.

"There must be another flaming breakdown," the man next to her said.

"There must," she answered. She didn't like him, and had no desire whatsoever to talk to him—he had a red and bulbous nose that spoke of drink—but she didn't want to be rude.

There was a distant roll of approaching thunder.

"Here it is," said strawberry-nose. "A bit of luck. Yesterday I was an hour late."

"The fog?" she asked politely.

"Nah—I overslept."

The thunder grew into a roar, mercifully ending the conversation. The white light, a dragon with a single eye, rushed towards them; it screeched past, thundering vengeance with a puff of foul breath, and it slithered to a halt. The doors slid open, the crowd surged forward carrying her with them, and there she was, jostled on every side by these rancid, furtive-eyed creatures of the underworld. She held on to a strap for dear life lest they should bowl her over and crush her.

"Five minutes late—not too bad," Strawberry-nose muttered in her face.

She smelt his toothpaste and turned her head, wanting to avoid it, and avoid the sight of those enlarged pores, and the ill-shaven upper lip. She hated such things, yet they hurt, reminding her of things she wanted to forget. For even if she admitted a sense of loss without Herbert, how could she get him back when he was already on the high seas to a new continent? It was too late now to repent.

As if to taunt her, immediately in front of her a short little woman with a pasty face and a shock of ringlets like a French poodle clung on to the lapel of an ugly, middle-aged man with a long, pointed nose, and a nasty, straggling moustache over a grin of discoloured teeth. This absurdly hideous pair were absorbed in each other, staring into each other's bloodshot eyes like lovers in a film about Paris, and breathing on to each other like dogs on street corners. It was horrid. If she and Herbert would behave like that, it was far better that the story should end with them separating while they each had some shred of dignity and privacy left.

Someone groaned. She looked round to see who it was . . .

"Are you all right?" Strawberry-nose asked.

"Yes, yes, thank you," she said bewildered. It must have been *her* making that idiotic noise. How odd! Why? Because something in her didn't *want* to live in solitary dignity, separated for ever from Herbert? Because the thought of their friendship resolving itself into a desultory correspondence—like hers with Daddy— was intolerable? She had a vision of herself writing letters like Miss Pritchard, huddled in an overcoat for the cold—and her letters, too, would receive no answer. Herbert would find another girl to marry him. Her only compensation would be a privacy as hygienic as solitary confinement in a hospital after an operation, a privacy that would end only with death.

She groaned again, unable to help it, and she cast around desperately for some relief. But there was none. She was dying, and she had chosen death. She could only blame herself.

The poodle woman and her man were alive, breathing as they were into each other's faces. Nola and Rudi were alive. Even Strawberry-nose, holding in his right hand a *Daily Express* neatly folded into a square, was alive. His strap-hanging hand wore a wedding ring, which meant, no doubt, a frowzy little wife washing up the breakfast things, and two children, perhaps, just filing out of morning prayers into their classrooms.

All these people were alive because they were involved with each other—the poodle and her boy-friend, Strawberry-nose and his family, Nola, Gladys, Norma, and so on. They all had other people to think about, and work for, and (presumably) complain about, while she had no one. There was only herself in her neat little tomb.

Why? Because she allowed herself to get hysterical at the smell of a human being. Human beings, like animals, had their particular odour, so she scorned contact with them. Bradshaw smelled of talcum powder only because he was not real.

The reality of Bradshaw was Herbert Bacon, and he had a real smell, and real needs. Like a child, he needed her—for who would take care of such a battered little man if she didn't? To use the imagination to escape the responsibility of Bradshaw alive and kicking, and eating and drinking and, yes, sweating, to a dream Bradshaw, a Bradshaw who never spoke till he was asked, who always disappeared when he was a nuisance, who had no needs other than her own, was despicable. The only right use of imagination was to try and make the live Bradshaw happier—and not only him, but all human creatures, no matter in how small a way. To despise and fear men and women—and animals, too, for that matter, was to despise and fear God. To live alone, voluntarily substituting a childhood vision for the love of a real person, was truly to live in sin. The only goodness lay in the giving of herself, as best she could, to other people. Like poodle-head hanging on to her man's lapel as if he were Clark Gable—and perhaps making him feel as if he were, for all his long nose and brown teeth. Like Strawberry-nose talking to her for the sake of a little human companionship, because it was a nasty day and a little friendly conversation might brighten up the morning a little.

She turned to him, trying to catch his eye.

"Isn't this a horrid journey?" she whispered.

"What?" he said, looking up from his racing results.

"Isn't it a horrid journey?" she repeated.

"Oh, shocking," he said, "but you usually travel by bike, don't you?"

"Yes," she answered in astonishment. "How do you know?"

"I work in the same building as you. Aren't you one of the typists with Boothby, Gold's?"

She nodded.

"Well, I'm a sorting clerk opposite you. I've always wanted to listen to you girls talking—you seem to be 'aving a proper hen party. And you're always making yourselves tea—you do yourselves well, don't you?'

She recalled Herbert with a little twist of longing and smiled.

"Come and have a cup of tea with us some time," she said, "and we'll do our best to do you well, too."

III

"Good morning Nola, good morning Mrs Sneath, good morning Norma."

"Good morning," the three murmured.

"You are well this morning, no?" Nola asked. "I have what you call a hangover."

"I had," Margaret admitted, "but it's better now. I'll make you a good cup of tea then you'll feel better. Headache?"

"Ye-es," Nola smiled. "I am no longer a chicken, yes? Today I could eat no breakfast, but when I was the age of Norma, I could dance and drink wine all night, and eat breakfast like a horse."

"Whatever were you two doing?" Norma asked. "Did you 'ave a party or suthink?"

"Yes, Norma," said Nola, massaging her forehead. "We drank some German wine that Rudi brought. I get you and your Johnny a bottle for your wedding, no?"

"Thanks, ever so," said Norma, grinning, "but I dunnow as I want it, judging from you two."

"Were you celebrating your engagement to Mr Bradshaw, Miss Finlay?" Gladys needled.

There was a silence.

"In a way," said Margaret. "Nola helped me make up my mind to go after him."

"Where to?" Gladys sneered. "To Hollywood, I s'pose, or Timbuctoo, maybe."

"To the ends of the earth," said Margaret. "To wherever he chooses to go, as long as he wants something that I can give him."

"Oh, reely, Miss Finlay," said Gladys, "you talk like *Woman's Own*."

"Yes, I suppose I do," said Margaret.

Did she mean it that she would follow him to Canada? that

she would give up her dear little room to voyage to a strange land? But that was a dreadful prospect—Ebury Street derelict, Ebury Street with a strange occupant, and she in a strange room in a strange city in a distant land. And what if when she got there Herbert had found some other girl? There would be no Nola there to comfort her, and no dear, familiar little room to retreat to, to shut the door on a hostile world.

It was a chance she must take. She must make this pilgrimage to a new land in order to find Bradshaw the reality, in order to give him what she could, and fulfill her destiny. If the worst happened, and Herbert no longer wanted her—which was what she deserved—she must find someone else to whom to give. Surely, there were lots of lonely people, frightened people—as Nola had said—who were longing for a little human warmth and companionship. Surely she need never live solitarily again, except by sinful choice.

The telephone rang.

"Typists' room," said Nola—"yes, she is here. Margaret, it's for you."

Margaret's heart jumped.

"Margaret Finlay speaking." Her voice had gone as breathless as if she were swimming.

"It's me, Herbert Bacon. I just thought I'd say no hard feelings and good luck." His voice was curt, but just as she remembered it.

"I wanted to say that to you—and much more. I've sent you a letter—can you hear me?"

The phone was crackling.

"Watcha say?" He sounded as if he was at the bottom of a well.

"I said I've sent you a letter," Margaret shouted. "I wanted to apologize. You see it was all untrue about my being engaged to someone else. I went a bit crackers, that's all. I said things I didn't mean."

"You mean you aren't engaged to Bradshaw!" He sounded incredulous.

"You're Bradshaw, don't you see? Only I got frightened and made a mistake. I'm a terrible fool, but I couldn't help it. Will you let me come to Canada—please? I'll never be such a nit-wit again, I promise."

There was a buzzing like a vacuum cleaner—what on earth was he saying?

"Margaret lass, *will* you marry me?"

"Did you ask me to marry you?"

"Aye. Will you marry me? I'll not ask again, mind."

"Yes, oh, yes, if you'll have me."

"Gor—what shall I do, lass? The ship sails in an hour—it was delayed for the fog. What d'you want me to do? Should I miss it and come after you?"

"No, no, catch it. It's silly to waste the passage when we'll need every penny. I'll come out and join you as soon as I can get a passage. You're sure you want me? Can you really forgive me?"

"I'll show you I've forgiven you the very moment I have you in me arms," he said. "I'll wire you as soon as I arrive. Write to me—write care of Cunard, Montreal. Oh, Margaret! You've never told me where you live!"

"Eighty Ebury Street," she shouted, "London, S.W.1. Have you got that?"

"Right you are," he said, "Eighty Ebury Street, S.W.1.—I've got it, lass. And you're engaged, understand. No more tomfoolery with Bradshaw, nor with anyone else, see?"

"Whatever you say," she said.

The operator interrupted them.

"That's three minutes, caller. If you want longer time, please insert two shillings and threepence."

"All right, Margaret lass, there's no point in wasting our brass.

Please God, I'll see you me wife soon."

"*Bon voyage*," she called. "I'll be with you by Christmas, even if I have to fly."

"God speed," he said, sounding rather choked.

"And God speed you, my darling," she cried.

The phone clicked and went dead. She handed the receiver back to Nola, smiling while the tears ran down her cheeks. She felt as glad and as fearful as a mother with a new-born child.

"Thank you, Nola," she said; "thank you with all my heart."

"I am delighted," said Nola. "Congratulations, my dear."

"Cor," breathed Norma, "you sounded just like a movie. Was that Bradshaw?"

"It sounded to me rather like Mr Bacon," Gladys jeered.

"One and the same thing," Margaret said calmly.

"You told us a lot of lies about him, didn't you?" Gladys snarled. "You made it all up about him being a film star, didn't you?"

"Yes," said Margaret, "I'm afraid I lied to everyone a bit, including myself. You must forgive me—I meant no harm."

"My dear," said Nola, "marriage is not easy either—you know this?"

"I know," said Margaret, "and I'm terribly scared. But it can't be more wretched than living in sin—can it? I've been living in sin ever since I was eight years old. It's about time he made an honest woman of me."

About the Author

Peter Lawrence Marchant was born May 14, 1928 in London, England. During World War II, he was sent to Uppingham, a boarding school in the country, to escape the London Blitz. He spent one year at University College London, studying Economics, acting in the school's drama society, and writing. Two of his short plays from this time were accepted by the BBC. Failing his exams at age 18, he joined the British Army and was assigned to the Royal Army Educational Corps, where he discovered his lifelong love of teaching.

Following his military service, he spent a year in London working for his father as an apprentice rubber-market clerk, before entering the University of Cambridge's Gonville & Caius College, where he studied History and English. After graduating, he moved to Canada in 1954, where he taught English at the University of British Columbia in Vancouver before enrolling in the Ph.D. program at the University of Iowa. It was there that he met his future wife, the Arkansas novelist Mary Elsie Robertson. After earning his Ph.D. and publishing his thesis novel *Give Me Your Answer, Do*, his academic specialty became the 19th-Century British Novel, which he taught at Penn State and the State University of New York, Brockport. His dedication to teaching earned him the Excellence in Teaching Award.

During the Vietnam War, Dr. Marchant was active in the peace movement and joined the Religious Society of Friends in the 1970s, becoming an active Quaker. Later in his career, he became interested in the stories and experiences of the survivors of the Holocaust. Even after partially retiring, he continued to teach one class a semester—the Literature of the Holocaust. Through that class, and working with director Steven Spielberg's Survivors of the Shoah Visual History Foundation, he got to know a large contingent of Holocaust survivors, helping several of them write their own memoirs. He continued teaching memoir classes after he and his wife retired to Winslow, Arkansas, in 2005. Dr. Marchant passed away on October 26, 2013.

Acknowledgments

The publisher extends his profound thanks to the following for their generous financial support which helped to defray some of this edition's production costs:

Alan J Abrams, Kevin Adams, E Andi Anderson,
Thomas Young Barmore Jr, Kian S. Bergstrom, Sam Bertram,
Alfred C. Bie, Brad Bigelow (The Neglected Books Page),
Brian R. Boisvert, Bonriguez, Ashley Bray,
Shannon Leigh Broughton-Smith, Barry Buchanan,
Michael Burten, Chris Call, Michael C. Cantelon,
Captain Awesome, Scott Carlson, Scott Chiddister,
Shelby Churchill, Chelsea Clifton, Greg Cobb, Joel Coblentz,
Costa, Donna Cousins, Violet Jijing Covey,
Parker & Malcolm Curtis, Robert Dallas, dcmalone,
Frank Derfield Jr., Dylan & Sam Doomwarre, V.M. Downey,
Isaac Ehrlich, Myrhat Eliot, Curtis B. Edmundson,
Stephen Fuller, Jamie Gallagher, Justin Gallant, Pierino Gattei,
Stephan Glander, Elise G., GmarkC, Gary Goff, B F Gordon Jr,
David Greenberg, Aric Herzog, Dave Holets, J. Holmes,
Trainor Houghton-Whyte, Izzy Huddleston, Ben Jacobson,
Martin Jarvis, Derek Jellison, Erik T Johnson, Fred W Johnson,
Kaitlyn A. Johnston, Addison Jones, Josh(qhool), Rebekah Kass,
Kate Alyssa, Kurt Johann Klemm, Kyle, C. Labairon,
James Latzer, Janine Lawton, Leonore the Wanderer,
Peyton Light, Gardner Linn, Nick Long, Elizabeth A Martinez,

Jim McElroy, Donald McGowan, Ian McMillan, Jack Mearns, William Messing, Jason Miller, JL Mock, Sherry Mock, Spencer F Montgomery, Steven Moore, A.L. Morgan, Gregory Moses, Scott Murphy, Clyde Nads, Naticia, Michael O'Shaughnessy, Joseph Alexander Onifer, Andrew Pearson, Dakotah Petty, Julie Phillips, zasu pitts, Pedro Ponce, Chase Pritchard, Ned Raggett, Judith Redding, Ryan C. Reeves, Kay Reindl, T. Richert, Robert Riley-Mercado, Franziska Rück, Oliver S, Rebecca S, George Salis (www.TheCollidescope.com), David W. Sanderson, Florian Schiffmann, Ethan Schmidt, James C. Schoech, Katherine Shipman, Kelly Snyder, Yvonne Solomon, Elijah Kinch Spector, Martin Stein & Scott Saxon, Stitches, K. L. Stokes, Stephen Michael Tabler, Taylor Ann, Tousedsa, Elisa Townshend, Sydney Umaña, Christopher Wheeling, Isaiah Whisner, Charles Wilkins, T.R. Wolfe, Keelyn Wright, Natalia Yamrom, Karen Young, Your Name Here, Yusa, The Zemenides Family, and Anonymous